TEXAS *Gift*

RJ SCOTT

TEXAS GIFT

TEXAS SERIES, BOOK 8

RJ SCOTT

Love Lane Books

For every reader who wanted to find out what happened to Jack, Riley, and their family.

And always for my family.

A PERSONAL NOTE FROM RJ

In the past few weeks the community has lost two people that impacted my life.

First, Stacia Hess, a constant cheerleader, and one of my trusted proofers.

I missed you when I sent out the files for this book.

Second, Sandrine Gasq Dion, who left us suddenly.

I'll miss your smiling face.

CHAPTER 1

*R*iley needed to apologize. Right *now*.

He'd fucked up big time, and he should have seen it coming, because everything he did went in cycles. He and Jack hadn't argued in so long. Maybe the tension that had been building inside Riley had needed an outlet; he'd provoked the argument. He'd pushed and prodded and sulked and shoved at Jack until Jack had snapped.

Not in loud shouting temper, or anything like what Riley deserved. No, Jack had gone deathly quiet.

Absolutely. Utterly. Quiet.

Riley shouted at him, got everything out of his system, felt the weight of it all lessen by throwing it at Jack, and what had happened? He'd stood there at first, confused, and then steadily calmer. Weirdly calm.

They argued; no normal marriage went without arguments over things as important as the kids or as trivial as picking up wet towels. But they resolved things, Jack/Riley was a unit that worked. They sometimes bickered and teased, they rarely shouted, and on the odd occasion there would be sulking. Mostly from Riley. He considered it as *thinking time* but Jack just called him on his sulking like a child.

Their arguments always ended in love; talking, kissing, complete forgiveness that could only come when two people understood and loved each other.

This morning though, Riley had made Connor cry, Lexie scowl, and caused Max to hide under the table with Toby. Jack hadn't even stayed for that—the crying, scowling and hiding had happened after he'd left.

"Why are you shouting at Pappa!" Connor shouted back at Riley. "Stop shouting." Then he'd started to cry.

Riley's heart had broken into a million pieces. He'd sat between a crying Connor and a sullen, angry Lexie and tried to explain that he had a bad headache and he didn't mean to shout. For headache, read migraine, tight painful migraine that blurred his vision and made him feel sick. He'd taken meds and the sharp edges of the glass in his head were easing, but he couldn't think straight. Connor stopped crying.

"You were so mean," Lexie summarized, but she did give Riley a hug and kissed him on the forehead to make it all better.

Max on the other hand, while not angry with Riley and the shouting, was still under the kitchen table with Toby. The black lab, Riley's black lab, lay between Max and Riley in a protective furry wall.

"It's okay Tobes, I got this," Riley tried to fold all six-four of himself under the wood tabletop. He got caught on a bench, his neck burned, his stomach was in knots, but nothing was going to stop him from getting to Max. Toby did eventually move to one side but not too far. Toby may have well been Riley's dog initially, but he and Max were inseparable now.

"Max, buddy?" he began, and Max at least looked up at him for a split second. "You okay?"

"M'okay," Max said. "You're noisy."

At least he wasn't rocking, or stimming. He was just sitting with his dog in his favorite place under the kitchen table.

"Is everything okay?" Carol said from behind him. He scrambled back and brushed himself off. "Riley?"

"I shouted," Riley explained simply.

"At the kids?" Carol asked, aghast, as if that was the ultimate sin in her eyes. Which, to be fair, it was in Riley's as well. He and Jack didn't shout, they cajoled, and bargained, and ran a happy house. Most of the time, anyway. Just not this morning.

"No, at Jack."

"Is Max okay?" She peered under the table and smiled at Max. He adored her, the kids all loved their nanny, probably quite a bit more than they loved their dad today.

"He seems fine." Riley peered out of the window at where Jack had gone. The damage had been done, but Connie and Lexie were chatting to each other, Max was with Carol and he needed to go and make things right with Jack.

"I think we're okay in here," Carol said, "Go find Jack."

Riley shot her a grateful glance, and as he left the kitchen he heard Lexie telling Carol that her Daddy had a headache and that she'd kissed it better. When he closed the door it was just him and the ranch and finding Jack. It didn't take him long; he was outside their barn, looking up at the siding, with his feet apart and his arms crossed over his chest.

Riley inhaled the fresh morning air and pulled back his shoulders. He could do this; he could ignore the pain in his head now it had lessened a little, he could push back nausea, and he could go and apologize to Jack for being a fucking idiot.

"I'm sorry," he murmured, coming to a stop next to Jack, only a few inches separating their arms. Jack didn't move.

"It's okay." Although it didn't sound okay at all. Okay was one of those words that meant nothing in the context of an argument, it was a word that plastered over cracks in a relationship. Okay was quiet and tight-lipped silences and Riley recalled *okay* from when he was a kid.

He hated okay.

"It's not okay, I have a headache and I didn't mean any of what I said."

"You didn't mean to say that life would be easier if you didn't have to listen to me?" Jack's voice was low and serious, and Riley winced.

"You were saying too much, and I couldn't think."

Their discussion had started in the bedroom.

"I asked if you'd made an appointment to see someone about the headaches."

"I know—"

"And why you were limping again—"

"Jack—"

"And why you weren't sleeping, and why you spent so much time at the office, and why the fuck have we not used the barn in over a month?"

The barn wasn't just *the barn*, it was a euphemism for sex. They hadn't been together in a month, over a month now. How did Riley explain that he'd been at the office, sometimes with the blinds shut, closing out the light, sleeping? How did he explain he didn't want to see a doctor because the headaches scared him? And how the hell did he tell Jack he was limping because every single one of his muscles hurt, because he was tired, because it was all too much?

"Jack, I'm sorry."

"You're not, Riley, because you won't listen to me." Jack

pointed at the barn. "I'm thinking we turn this into a game room for the kids."

Riley gripped Jack's arm. "No, what the hell?" His tension fled and in its place was panic. This was *their* space. Sometimes they came out here to talk, to hide away from the world, but it was also the one place they had the hottest sex he'd ever experienced. He wanted that again, but he was so tired, every time he turned over in bed his neck hurt, and his head pounded, and his leg ached, and he was fucking tired of it all. "Jack, I'm sorry, don't…"

Jack turned to face him. "Either you go to the doctor, right here, right now, or I start clearing the place for a pool table." He looked dead serious, and Riley couldn't tell if this was an empty threat. Then Jack softened, cradled his face and pressed a kiss to his forehead. "Riley, please."

Just those two words pierced the fear in Riley, he couldn't stop the pain, or the threat of being sick, or not sleeping, but whatever was wrong, Jack would be there for him.

"I'm scared," Riley murmured.

Jack gathered him close. "You think I'm not?"

"Please don't," Riley said against Jack's neck. His words sounded slurred and fear made him sway. *What the hell?* "Please don't let me chase you away."

"I won't."

And that was the last thing he heard as his world went black.

CHAPTER 2

*J*ack held Riley's hand. It wasn't much but it was all he could do. The rest of it, getting him to the hospital, the doctors poking at him, Riley pretty much out of it, that was all out of Jack's hands.

And now he had to listen to the whys, after the MRI scan and with Riley in and out of sleep. He had to sit here and listen to a doctor explain to him what had happened. The words were muddled, but Josh was here with him, and Eden, and they flanked him in the room as he held Riley's hand.

Riley wore a neck brace and was asleep, finally free from the headaches that had been plaguing him. His doctor, a thin wiry man who was attempting to explain the issues at hand, was wording things to keep Jack calm.

"Cervical spinal stenosis is diagnosed when degenerative changes in the cervical spine cause spinal cord compression," he began. "The spinal cord is a nerve bundle that runs from the base of the brain to the lower back." He turned an iPad with a 3D image of a spine rotating and then pressed an arrow. This time the images were cross-sectional. "In a normal spine, there is more than enough room for the spinal cord in the spinal canal, but what we see here in this case is that with his cervical spinal stenosis, space becomes too narrow. The spinal cord is a critical component for sending signals all over the body, which would explain the pain in his previously injured leg."

"And you know for sure this is what my brother has?" Eden asked, composed, even though Jack had seen the worry in her eyes. Riley and Eden were so close, brought up in an environment of entitlement and hostility.

"We carried out a detailed exam, and the MRI simply confirmed our initial diagnosis."

All Jack could think was that he was grateful Riley had been sedated for the MRI; Jack couldn't imagine being in such a tightly confined space.

"Okay, so what else?" Jack asked when Doctor Edwards checked back at his notes.

"The neurological deficits that the patient has been experiencing—"

"Riley," Jack interrupted, "his name is Riley."

Doctor Edwards nodded. "The effects that Riley has been experiencing, resulting from the spinal cord compression, is a condition called myelopathy."

"And this was all because of that accident in Nuevo Laredo?" Josh asked the question Jack wanted to ask but didn't know how. He needed to understand why this had happened, and the suggestion that a trauma caused the whole thing gave Jack something to blame.

"Or the incident with the horse and the fire," Eden interjected. She and Josh exchanged glances.

"Either incident could be to blame," Doctor Edwards said. "Cervical stenosis with myelopathy tends to get slowly worse over time, the initial injury could have affected his spine and been missed, or maybe it wasn't so bad initially and has worsened. There is always variation. Symptoms can remain stable for long periods or rapidly worsen, it depends on the patient involved."

"So what now?"

"In most cases the first course of action is physical therapy, aided by epidural injections to allow realignment of the affected area, but I think that in Riley's case, the first option would be to operate."

Jack's didn't want to hear that, he didn't want to know that this was anything worse than some shit like food poisoning. He tightened his hold on Riley's hand for a moment and Riley moved his head, but didn't open his eyes. He was still sleeping the sleep of the dead.

Jesus, Jack, why the hell are you using words like that?

"But we could try nonsurgical treatments first? Right?" Jack said, and he knew he sounded panicked, feeling only reinforced when Eden leaned into him and Josh put a steadying hand on his shoulder.

Doctor Edwards placed the iPad on the bed, right next to the notes.

"In rare cases, the symptoms of myelopathy can be mild enough we could go the nonsurgical route. However, because of the risk of severe nerve damage, you can ask any surgeon and they'll recommend an operation to relieve the pressure on the spinal cord."

Jack attempted to unknot the tension inside. He had to be the strong one here, the one who could handle everything that happened to Riley. The one able to make the decisions for him.

"What would the next steps be?" he asked, even though he didn't want to hear it at all.

"We'll be taking more scans, but from my assessment and that of my surgical colleague we are looking at anterior cervical decompression and fusion. Simply put, this procedure involves approaching the cervical spine from the front and removing any discs, bone spurs, or other structures that might be impinging the spinal cord."

That doesn't sound simple at all.

The doctor paused for a moment and picked up the model of the spine he'd brought with him. He flexed the model and began to talk, but to Jack it was all a blur. "It typically includes fusing one or more levels of the cervical spine to maintain stability. He will wear a neck brace post-op, and there will be a good four weeks of recovery time, some of which will be here in this hospital."

"Our bedroom is downstairs," Jack blurted out, horribly aware that everyone was looking at him as if he'd lost his mind. "So, that makes it easy for him to come home."

I want him to come home.

Doctor Edwards nodded, whether that was in agreement or just acknowledgment of what Jack had said, it was not certain.

He asked if there were any more questions, and Jack was sure he would think of so many once the doctor had walked out of the room. Right now, though, he just wanted to know.

"Will he be okay?"

"The usual statistics about operations in and around the spine apply, but your husband is young and strong and there is every hope that this will be successful and with therapy he will be absolutely fine."

Was it weird that out of all that Jack focused on the word hope? The doctor *hoped* that Riley would be okay.

He could hold onto that hope in a negative way, where Riley died or was paralyzed, or he could take the word hope and turn it on its head. He refused to let the faith he had in what the doctors could do and tarnish it with terror.

So he took *hope* and held it close.

Right next to his heart.

When Riley woke next, Jack was the only one in the room. Hayley was flying in today and he'd told Eden and Josh they should go and pick her up, get out of the hospital, get some air. They argued, but Jack wasn't leaving Riley. Not for anything.

"Wha'appened?" Riley's voice was gravelly, and Jack focused on hazel, bloodshot eyes, and the slurred words. He leaned over and helped Riley with a drink of water, then scooted his chair a little closer so he could hold Riley's hand again.

"You have a problem with your neck," he explained, deciding the word spine was one step too far. "It gave you the headaches, and explained the problems with your leg."

Riley looked at him from the corner of his eye, then from him to the ceiling, blinking up at the tiles. He didn't say anything.

"Bad?" he asked.

"Not so much," Jack lied. "Small op and you'll be back home."

And the worst of this? Riley closed his eyes again, and let out a small sigh. What Jack said had reassured him, even though he'd been lying.

When Riley woke the next time he appeared more coherent, the time after that he asked to sit up, but still Jack didn't tell him the whole truth.

Hayley arrived a little after four in the afternoon. She'd been in New York with her school, and had demanded to come home as soon as she'd heard what had happened. How could Jack say no, Riley would want her here, and so did he.

Jack stood and hugged her. Was it possible she'd gotten taller in the three weeks she'd been away? Or maybe something made her look more grown up, or maybe it was just because she was calm.

"Oh, Pappa," she said. "What happened?"

Jack wanted simple words to explain to their daughter the terror he felt, and the pain Riley had been in, and the fact that he needed an operation. He was the one who faced things head-on, who didn't panic, but right now he was not doing well at all.

"He collapsed."

She moved to the other side of the bed and pressed a kiss to Riley's head, then took his other hand, careful of the cannula there.

"I know that, but why? What did the doctors say?"

Jack didn't want to do this, but Hayley was eighteen and she had a right to be treated like an adult. "His spinal cord is compressed, he needs an operation to free the space so it isn't so tight." That was how he'd understood the situation and he hoped he was right in what he was saying.

"An operation on his spine?" Hayley slid into the chair, still holding Riley's hand.

That he couldn't lie about at all. "Yes."

"Is it dangerous…," she began, and then shook her head, "of course it's dangerous. What did dad say about it?"

"I'm not sure he understands yet, I'll talk to him when he next wakes up. He'll be happy you're here."

"Of course," Hayley said, and then she began to cry. Not sobbing, just quiet tears that broke Jack's heart.

"He'll be okay, sweetheart."

Jack couldn't let himself think otherwise.

HAYLEY SLEPT, THE HOSPITAL WAS QUIET, AND A PARADE OF family had visited Riley today. He'd seemed brighter, able to talk and laugh, albeit with a wince every so often.

"The drugs are good," he'd joked every time he'd been asked how the pain was.

Jack was as exhausted as Hayley looked. This was day

three and tomorrow, all being well, the operation would be underway. A quick in and out, the surgeon called it, dismissing concerns with a bright cheeriness that contradicted the somber mood in the room. Riley had taken everything in; every tiny detail. He'd heard the odds, listened to the explanation, even smiled when he was told that this would probably fix all his issues. Only when the surgeon had gone, after a firm handshake and a cheery *see you in the morning* did Riley go quiet. Hayley curled up in the spare chair and fell asleep, so it was just Jack and Riley awake in this room.

"She's beautiful isn't she?" Riley said, and Jack looked up from the hand in his lap. Last he'd noticed, Riley had been as fast asleep as Hayley was. "Hayley, I mean."

Jack studied their daughter as objectively as he could, but he was so biased about all four of their children. They were all gorgeous and funny and bright and blessed. Hayley had her dad's hair and eyes and she was already five-ten, she might well get taller, who knew. She was so like Riley; in fact he was a mini-Riley, with his spark and drive, and Jack loved her so much.

"She is." Jack moved to get Riley some more water. When he'd done that he went to sit again in the hard chair, but Riley patted the bed.

"Come here," he said. Jack didn't argue, anything that got him closer to Riley was a good thing. He sat, taking care not to lean too far so it rolled Riley. "I love you." He found Jack's hand, lacing their fingers.

"And I love you," Jack replied, pressing a kiss to Riley's forehead.

"If anything happens to me tomorrow—"

"Nothing will happen." Jack believed wholeheartedly in the power of positive thinking and he wouldn't let Riley's normal default stress setting railroad this whole thing.

But, there was no stress, or panic, or pessimism in Riley's expression.

"*If* something happens," he began again in that tone that defied Jack's any attempt to talk over him when he had something important to say. "Tom knows what is happening at CH. I think he'd be a good person to keep there to run the place."

"Riley—"

"And, my will, everything goes to you, you know that."

Emotion choked Jack, stopping his breath. "I know," he said, because Riley didn't look as if he was in the mood for arguments.

"I don't want you to work at CH, okay, I don't want that as my legacy, I want you to go on doing what you're doing. CH will be okay. The kids? I couldn't be prouder of them, you tell them that if…okay, you tell them."

A tear slipped out of Riley's eye and trickled down his cheek, sliding to the pillow.

"Please, Riley."

"You promise me you'll find someone else, okay Jack—?"

Jack reached his limit, leaning right down and kissing Riley. "Shut. The. Hell. Up." Riley didn't have any choice in the matter. "I'm not listening to this."

"That's stupid—"

"No Ri, that is unshakeable faith and love."

CHAPTER 3

*R*iley wondered, in his drugged-up state, if it was possible to fit more people in the room.

The post-operative recovery area teemed with people, or at least it seemed that way, and not ones he wanted in the room like Jack or the kids or family. No, these were interns and nurses measuring heart rate, blood pressure, and respiration, and making not-so-helpful comments about pain reflex. There were all kinds of them asking him stupid questions when all he wanted was to see a friendly face.

Jack.

He wanted Jack, right here next to him in this room. He must have said so, because a whole bunch of faces were right there telling him he was going back to his bed, and wasn't it good that everything was a success, and for him not to worry.

Well, he was worried damn it. And thirsty, and tired, and floating, and Jack should have been allowed into the recovery area.

Someone needed to be listening to him.

At last, they moved him, and he closed his eyes under the dizzying lights, waiting for the motion to stop.

"Hey." Was the first thing he heard—Jack's voice, and blame it on the meds or on his state of mind, or a desperate need to have Jack near him, but he cried.

By the end of that day it seemed as if the world and his wife had visited, but what he most anticipated was the kids coming in; the twins had a gift for him, apparently, and Max wanted to tell him a story about a tomato.

"How's the pain, Mr. Campbell-Hayes?" the latest nurse to check on him asked.

"I don't feel anything," Riley answered. He was so drugged-up it was doubtful he'd feel a baseball on his head.

The nurse made notes on his pad, and stood to one side when a doctor came in.

"How are we doing, Mr. Campbell-Hayes?"

"Fine," Riley said, because they expected him to say that. He caught Jack's quirk of a smile and tried not to smile himself. Jack had already warned him not to fake feeling okay to get home earlier than he should.

The damn man knew him too well.

"Nurse will fit you with a brace, and you should be out of here in one to two days."

"One," Riley insisted.

"One to two," the doctor corrected him. "And we'll furnish you with the appropriate discharge instructions. You may need help with daily activities like dressing and showering for the first few weeks. Fatigue is common. Let pain be your guide."

Riley was pretty fixated on the idea of needing help in the shower and smiled at Jack, but Jack was serious now, as if he was listening to the list of things they could and couldn't do.

"You can shower by the weekend, that's four days from the surgery, okay?"

Him, Jack, in a shower. Hell yes. He might not be able to go to his knees but Jack could.

"—recovery takes between four to six weeks."

"Riley?" Jack interjected, "are you listening?"

The doctor continued when Riley glanced back at him. "There will be targeted exercises with a Physical Therapist that'll last two to three months but I am sure that was covered in your pre-op assessment. Walk, a short distance at first, aiming eventually for up to two miles, and that will work on your body mechanics."

The doctor carried on, something about staples, or stitches, and Riley hoped Jack was taking notes because he was feeling some pain. Spikes of it in his shoulders and neck. He closed his eyes.

"You in pain Riley?" Jack asked.

"Uh huh," Riley murmured.

There was medication, and blessed relief, and the doctor left, meaning it was him and Jack in the room.

"When do the kids get here?" he asked when the fuzz of pain cleared a little.

"You sure you're up for that?"

"God yes."

"They're downstairs in the restaurant, I'll get them."

"You look really silly," Connor told Riley as soon as he walked into the room.

Lexie elbowed her brother. "Don't say that," she said in a loud whisper.

"Well he does look silly," Connor whispered back.

Jack corralled them closer to the bed, and Riley caught the nod he gave Lexie, who was making a really bad job of hiding something behind her back. He'd already seen the bright paper when she'd pushed Connor, but he didn't say a single word.

"We brought you this." Lexie thrust the gift out in front of her. "Pappa helped us 'cause of the glass."

"Don't tell him it's got glass, he'll know what it is." Now it was Connor's turn to elbow Lexie, but she ignored him. She mostly disregarded everyone and did her own thing.

Riley couldn't quite reach the gift, and patted the bed, waiting until Lexie and Connor had both climbed up, with some help from Jack. He made a great show, as much as he could with his clumsy hands and inability to look down, of opening the present and picked the frame up so he could see it closer.

The picture was one of him and Jack, with the kids on their shoulders; he had Connor, Jack with Lexie, and it had been taken on a day trip to the river. A beautiful day, Max had spent all of it finding the shiniest stones, and Hayley had only used her phone for taking photos. The whole day had been one of those shining, perfect moments in their lives and Riley looked straight at Jack to see his soft smile.

"I love this," he said to the twins, but also to Jack.

Lexie took it carefully from him and placed it on the bedside table, right next to the jug of water and the family cards.

"You can look at it later," she said, "when you can move your neck. Max has a present too, but he wanted to wait in the restaurant with Carol and Hayley and a huge pile of scrambled eggs." Lexie waved her hands expansively to indicate the quantity of egg. "I've never seen so much egg and then he put all this ketchup on it, loads and loads and loads, and it went all over the plate and some on the table. Hayley said it was okay though because he was quiet and happy, though Carol scooped some of it off and didn't know what to do with it, and Hayley had to get another plate."

Connor nodded along with his sister, but didn't have

anything to add. Although getting a word in edgeways when Lexie was on a streak was really hard.

The twins left with Carol and Max after Max explained that the ketchup at the hospital was yucky, and he wanted to go home. He didn't express anything like sympathy or affection, well not outwardly, but Riley hadn't been expecting it. Max stored away information and would talk about what had happened at some point. Carol explained Daddy was not well, that was all Max needed to know at this moment.

Hayley brought in snacks and drinks and sat cross-legged on the end of the bed, Jack pulled up a visitor's chair, turned it around and straddled it. Riley worried immediately, it didn't matter he was on meds and stuck in a bed, Hayley looked very serious and clearly had something on her mind.

"So, I wanted to talk to you guys, and it's important and scary," she began, halfway through an energy bar.

"We're listening," Jack offered, when Riley didn't say anything.

"I made a decision about college," she announced.

"I thought you were still looking at options."

"I was, but this is an easy decision, I know what I want, and I know where I want to be. I got accepted everywhere I'd applied but I've made a choice." She paused and Riley waited, expecting the lights to dim like on a talent show. Hayley had applied for a range of courses, from business to geology, but he'd never said a single word to influence her. This was her decision and she might love business school. Just because Riley didn't like it, didn't mean that Hayley would hate it as well.

"And?" Jack prompted. For someone who was usually so laid back the one thing he couldn't handle was suspense.

"I want to join the Geological Sciences program in Colorado."

Memories flooded Riley. He'd followed the family tradition and gone to a private college in upstate New York, studied business as his dad wanted; or rather he chose the only course his dad would fund. Given he didn't have access to his trust fund at that age and convinced he shouldn't have to work for money at that point in his life, he'd gone along with it. Coming out of the place with a shiny degree in business administration and a daughter he didn't know he'd created.

He'd have given anything to be studying geosciences, that was still his passion.

"What do you think, Dad?" Hayley asked when Riley hadn't said a word.

"Maybe your dad needs to sleep," Jack explained.

"No." Riley held up a hand. "I'm so proud of you, and so pleased that is what you want to do, but do you truly want to study Geology?"

Hayley nodded. "Remember that time you helped me with homework and you found those stones on the ranch? We went out on the horses, I was twelve, I think."

"Yeah, I remember that."

"We found topaz. And you explained it was a silicate mineral of aluminum and fluorine. And then you told me about the orthorhombic system, remember?"

"You remember all that?"

"Yep," she said proudly. "I wrote it all down and researched it."

"Even the bit about the crystals being mostly prismatic, terminated by pyramidal and other faces?"

Hayley grinned at him. "Yep, all of it. It's fascinating. That's where it started, and I want to work at CH if I'm good enough and help you research."

Riley's eyes stung with unshed tears, he couldn't have been prouder, or more blown away.

She clambered up the bed a little, fitting in next to Riley, "so you need to get better, Dad, so we can work together."

Riley planned on it. "I will."

Jack huffed a laugh. "Like father like daughter." He shook his head as he smiled, and Riley knew he was just as proud. "Don't go talking rocks around me," he added and faked a yawn. That earned him a greetings card in the face, and when it came time for Hayley to leave Riley realized he'd forgotten all the dark things, and that Hayley was a special kind of light in this family.

CHAPTER 4

*B*y the time they'd passed April and were firmly into May, Riley had ditched the collar and was working with a Physical Therapist, who spent a lot of time trying to make Riley cry. Or at least that's what Riley told Jack after every session.

"And then, Jesus, I had to bend to the right, and fuck, I could have cheerfully strangled the guy." Riley stomped around the kitchen, and yeah, stomping was the word Jack wanted to use. He was opening cupboards and shutting them again, and the poor cookie jar was perilously close to the edge of the counter. Jack rescued it and moved so he was between the cupboards and Riley, holding him still with a gentle touch on his arms.

"But you feel better?"

Riley stiffened to pull away and Jack rubbed patterns into his skin. Riley had been so brave in the hospital, had endured all kinds of pain and anxiety without a single word of complaint. But Jack couldn't fail to see that now Riley was feeling better he was impatiently in the wish-it-was-all-over stage. Riley leaned into him, pressing his face against Jack's and sighing.

"I just want this done."

Jack shifted so he could take Riley's weight and height at just the right angle and then slid a hand between them, unbuttoning Riley's jeans. At first Riley didn't get with the plan, still needing the hug. Then he seemed to realize what was happening and lifted his head from Jack's shoulder.

"Come on," Jack encouraged, "we can fool around a little, that's what the doc said."

At that Riley blushed, same as he had done when the doctor explained that relations, as long as they weren't too intense, could begin again. That had been two weeks ago, and they had made it to bed a couple of times, but it was always Riley getting Jack off, never Riley getting anywhere near orgasm.

"I can't," Riley murmured. "Not yet, still in too much pain."

Jack pulled back and looked Riley in the eyes. "Okay then," he said, determined, "get in the bedroom and you can suck me off."

Riley's eyes widened, but he didn't argue. He'd been very good about making sure that Jack was happy, that Jack got off, and fuck, it was starting to piss Jack right the hell off. This morning, no kids, no nanny, Robbie covering for him at the school, Vaughn out with the horses, this was his time to show Riley that he was getting better.

Of course, he wasn't doing this without research and one humiliating call to the same doc who said they could start to get it on.

As soon as they reached the bedroom he closed and locked the door. It didn't matter that no one was supposed to be home, it would be just their luck that someone would come looking for them. He could see the side of their barn from here, but that was for another day, when Riley was fully healed. Today was all about taking him out of himself and leaving him pliant and loose on the bed, all fucked out.

"Take off your clothes," Jack ordered. Riley hesitated, his hand on his belt. The three times he'd sucked Jack off since the doc's meeting he had been determined to keep his clothes on. "I mean it Riley."

Jack used his best I'm-in-charge voice, which sometimes made Riley hot, and sometimes made him laugh. Today he just looked confused, but at least he did as he'd been told. He stripped, fumbling over his belt and Jack watched until Riley was entirely naked, and then he copied him and dropped his clothes to the floor.

Riley had lost some weight in the hospital and during post-surgery, his muscles a little less defined, but god, he was gorgeous, from head to toe.

"On the bed," Jack commanded and Riley climbed onto the bed and scooted back so his ass was against the pillow. "No, lay down."

Riley slid down, awkwardly and slowly, and then lay back. Since the operation it wasn't that Riley had an issue with getting hard, his mental block was coming, tensing, and stretching his neck. When he'd first come home he'd slept in a recliner chair that Jack and Robbie had dragged in, and wore his cervical collar, and at least he was now sleeping in the same bed as Jack.

Jack climbed onto the bed and straddled Riley who frowned up at him.

"I'd be more comfortable on my knees." Riley gestured at the floor.

"That won't work," Jack said.

Riley looked puzzled, "I don't want to—"

"Shhh."

He rocked against Riley, their cocks aligned just right,

and then he circled both and gave them an experimental stroke together.

"No, Jack."

"The doc said this was fine. Relax."

"He didn't specifically—"

Riley stopped talking as Jack leaned over and sucked on his nipples, still lazily slipping his hand up and down their joined cocks. He loved tasting Riley, knew that his nipples were hardwired to his cock, in fact he knew a lot about Riley and his fears and what turned him on and what made him smile.

"I love you," he murmured against Riley's breastbone before he moved onto Riley's other nipple. Riley was rigid beneath him, until Jack tugged with his teeth and, almost unbidden, Riley's hands moved up to bury into Jack's hair.

There.

From that point on, Riley was lost. Jack could play this man like a fiddle, knew exactly where to kiss, and suck and bite, and he was still moving his hand. He sat back; Riley's eyes were shut but Jack needed them open, needed to see the lines on his body relax a little more. He released his hold on their cocks and then scooted up

"Feel," he ordered, taking Riley's hand and pressing it to his ass. It was all kinds of awkward in this position for him, but he made sure Riley didn't have to reach too far.

He knew when Riley felt that Jack had prepped himself, he let out a soft and low moan, and a single drawn-out *Jaaaackkk.*

"Push your fingers inside me." Jack had deliberately left lube within reach, and he had it in his hands. With Riley lost in exploration, Jack squirted out enough to make sure Riley's cock was good and covered. Then, in a smooth move, before Riley could even realize or protest, Jack moved back, knocking Riley's fingers out of the way, gripping his cock, and angling so he could slide himself on. The initial barrier, the discomfort lasted a moment as Jack relaxed and then Riley was inside, his expression one of bliss, his eyes shut again.

Jack rocked, his hands on Riley's chest, pressing down to stop Riley moving. "Open your eyes," Jack ordered. "Please," he added, when Riley didn't immediately do what he was told.

Riley's eyes opened, the hazel dark, and he was half smiling. "Hold me down," he murmured. "Don't let me arch up."

Jack was so with that plan, and he shifted his weight forward a little, Riley's cock angled and rubbing Jack's prostate. He was so close at just having Riley inside him, after so long, let alone the fact that the angle...

"Jeez," he muttered, the only coherent sound he could muster.

"Jack, god..." Riley moved and Jack pressed down, and Riley whined at that, "more."

Jack rotated his hips, pressed hard, pulled until there was so little of Riley inside, and then pushed back. Riley was so close, Jack could tell. He rocked some more, kept hold of Riley, and when Riley came he did it soundlessly, his mouth falling open, his eyes closing. Jack finished himself off in two quick tugs, already on edge, and eased off as best he could, finding a washcloth, expecting Riley to be angry with him.

But no. Cleaned up, Riley held out a hand and pulled Jack down next to him.

"You always get it," Riley said. "Doesn't matter how much I push, you never give up."

Jack smiled at him, then kissed him.

Then he thought teasing might be in order. "Not when sex is on the table anyway!"

They didn't move for a while, just content to be in each

other's arms. Jack loved their family, but sometimes it was nice for him and Riley to just be *them*.

Of course the peace didn't last, the first knock was Liam talking about a fencing issue which Jack answered. The second knock was Vaughn apologizing for Liam interrupting them. Jack didn't like to comment on the irony of that.

Then Riley's office called and while it wasn't urgent, it had both men up and out of bed.

"It was nice while it lasted," Riley said as he belted his jeans. Jack kissed away the pout, and the kiss lasted a hell of a long time.

The entire world could knock for them, or ring them, but nothing would make them stop kissing.

CHAPTER 5

*J*uly was a bitch. With it came the kind of heat that sucked you dry and left you crabby. A hurricane was heading for the south coast of Texas and causing the weather do some crazy shit; humidity alternating with storms. The main storm wouldn't reach them this far inland,; but even this distance from the center of the hurricane there was unpredictability about what each hour would bring. Riley had been tracking it on his PC, concerned about friends in Laredo, but so far everything was okay for them.

"You nearly done here?" Jack asked as Josh shoveled the last of the manure into the wheelbarrow and wiped the sweat off his face with his gloved hand.

"About done." He leaned the rake against the wall and stepped back to admire his work. "It's like riding a bike," he said, with a wide grin.

For some reason Josh had turned up this morning in old jeans, and a ragged T with his old Stetson and demanded to help Jack in the stables. They'd worked mostly in silence clearing out the barns, and Jack had given Josh his space.

Still, he'd taken him at his word that this was what he was there for, but he knew his brother well, and something was eating at Josh.

Jack tossed him a water bottle and waited, as he had done for the two hours since Josh had gotten there.

"So, there was something I wanted to talk to you about," Josh began, sitting on a crate by the open door in the shade.

Here it comes. *I won't worry until I've heard everything.*

"Yeah?" Jack asked. "Everything okay? With Anna? The kids?"

"Anna's good, Lea and Sarah as well...look... It's Logan I wanted to talk to you about."

Jack took a seat on the other crate and waited for Josh to explain. Logan had gone through some bad years, teenage stuff, some more serious than the rest, but he was in year three of pre-law up north and it seemed to Jack whenever he saw him that the kid was doing good.

"What about him?"

"He's been working at a law firm in the city, intern work experience type thing, but he's coming home, you know, for Hayley's birthday."

"I expected he would." The whole family would be there but it wasn't only Hayley's birthday. She was leaving for college soon, so it was a goodbye. Something Riley wasn't handling too well, particularly as he'd finished his therapy and felt as if he'd lost all of the last months to being ill. Didn't matter that Hayley had spent a long time with her Dad, reading and talking geology. She'd been the best medicine for Riley and had taken to doing the daily walks with him over to the school and back.

Josh stared at the bottle in his hands. "Logan's not happy, Jack."

"In what way?"

"His courses are going well, he's near the top of every

class, he has friends, but every chat we have he doesn't seem to be quite right."

"You want me to talk to him?"

Josh looked up at him then, and then shook his head. "It's Hayley."

"Hayley? Our Hayley?"

"I think he wants to give everything up to come home because of her."

Jack waited a moment before answering. Josh wasn't confrontational, but it sure seemed as though he was apportioning blame somewhere.

"What makes you think that?"

Logan keeps asking about Hayley, wanting to find just the right present for her birthday, and then as an afterthought he's all *I hate the city, I want to come home.* You tell me there isn't a correlation there, Jack."

Jack took a long, slow drink of water. "Okay," he began calmly, feeling that otherwise he might do a Riley and get protective of his daughter in a loud and physical way. This was his brother sitting opposite him and he was going to stay centered and not get defensive. "Have you thought that maybe Logan is not a city type?"

"He's in New York, you can't get a better place to be a lawyer. He has this chance and he's stupid not to use it."

"He's always said he wanted to work with you."

"In a backwater place like Selkirk and Unwin? Come on Jack, we want better for our kids."

Josh's expression spoke volumes; he was frustrated, and sad, and hopeful, all rolled into one, as in the Christmas he'd wanted a new bike and the one he got was secondhand. He'd been disappointed, and sad, but then he saw the possibilities and that was it, the bike was his.

Maybe he was different to Josh here, maybe having Max as a son, with all his needs and his quirky outlook on life had altered the way he looked at things. He wanted the best for his and Riley's kids, but he also wanted them to be happy.

That was it.

Happy.

Maybe this was the direction he should take with this conversation.

Jack cleared his throat. "I'm happy with my life, with the hard work, and the ranch, and my family. Are you happy?"

Josh blinked at him as if he couldn't wrap his head around the question his brother had asked. "Of course, I'm happy. Anna and the kids, my work, my place in the world, of course I'm happy."

"Would you be happier in New York at some fancy law firm?"

Josh looked shocked. "Not me, no, but Logan is different, you see that, right?"

"Not at all. I actually think Logan is just like his dad. He wants what he wants, and he'll get it whatever stands in his way."

Josh stood immediately and bristled. "Jesus, Jack, if this is some shit about how I left the ranch after dad died, and left you and Beth then I'm done talking to you."

Jack stood as well. "No, it isn't, if I look back at that time, I didn't resent you, and neither did Beth. We envied you, going off to college, learning what you needed, but I never resented it. I wanted to be here with the horses, this was my thing, hard work and pain, no money, and stress. I've always wanted it, because it means something to me."

"Then what is it you're saying?" Josh was toe-to-toe with him now, but he wasn't angry, he had a wild desperation in his eyes, as if he needed something to make everything right.

"That maybe when he comes home, you listen to what he says, and if it's a girl, or that he hates the city, or he wants to run off to join the circus, you listen to what makes him happy and everything will work out."

Josh stepped back and kicked at the crate which creaked with the force. "What's he going to do here, huh? Work with me?"

"Why not? You could start your own firm, Campbell and Campbell, father and son, and you know that if Lea or Sarah want to follow you into law, maybe they'd be happier here than in the city."

"But…what if it is Hayley? What if he makes decisions based on a girl? At his age? And not just any girl, but Hayley."

Jack valued his daughter, and if the implication was that she wasn't good enough for Logan then he would have punched his brother into the ground. But it wasn't. Not at all.

He had just one more thing to say on this. "You were twenty-two when you married Anna. You knew what love was then, right? You were happy, and you made decisions for your family that made sense. Let Logan do that for himself; find his own way."

Silence, Josh staring at the ground, but Jack waited. He'd learned that Josh was a thinker just as much as he was. Finally, Josh looked up.

"I love Hayley," he said. It was his way of apologizing, or making things clear, or some such nonsense that Jack didn't fully understand. He pulled Josh into a hug and they did the whole back patting thing, before separating.

"Are we done here?" Jack asked.

"Yeah, guess we are."

The noise of a truck outside the barn caught their attention, and both boys stepped forward when Neil Kendrick, their mom's husband, climbed down from the cab. The truck was stenciled with the name of his veterinary practice and he'd parked it skewed across the drive.

"Jack, I need your help," he said as soon as his boots hit dirt.

Fear had Jack darting forward, Josh on his tail. "Is it mom? What's wrong?" Jack imagined the worst, an accident, illness, but Neil stopped him in his tracks. He looked around himself as if he hadn't realized he'd arrived in such a dramatic way.

"I'm sorry, it's okay, nothing. Donna is fine."

Jack pressed a hand to his chest where his heart was beating way too fast and noticed Josh did something similar. Then another thought hit Jack.

"Is it you? Are you okay?" God, could he sound any more panicked?

"It's not me, look, I don't know where to start, but I think I need your help."

"What do you need me to do?" Jack asked, when it was obvious Neil was talking to him and not Josh.

"I have a friend, from veterinary school, Alec McGuire, he's working down in Liberty and he's in trouble. We need men, and horses, they're desperately trying to evacuate the animals with enormous difficulty because of the water, the hurricane and the flooding. He's right on the floodplain, outside of the Trinity National Wildlife Refuge. There are horses stuck, and livestock, and he wasn't asking, but I'm going down to help, and then I thought, some of those horses won't move, and Alec tells me there's some places under four feet of water."

Jack moved right into Neil's space, fully understanding what he was saying.

"It's okay," he said and gripped Neil's upper arms to get him to focus.

"Can you help?" Neil asked.

Jack wouldn't leave animals to suffer if he could help.

"Give me ten to get some stuff together, I'll come with you," he said.

He walked in on Riley doing some familiar exercises to strengthen his neck muscles. It might have been five months since the operation, but he was careful to follow to the letter everything the doctor and the Physical Therapist said to him.

"Hi," Riley said, as he caught sight of Jack in the mirror.

Jack hugged him from behind and kissed his cheek. "I have this thing," he said.

"I know." Riley smiled. "It's a very fine *thing*."

"No, wait," he launched into the reason he was here before Riley could say anything else, "Neil has a friend down in Houston."

Riley turned in Jack's arms, awkwardly. "Shit, is he okay? Is he flooded out?"

"He's a veterinarian," Jack said, and no, that didn't answer Riley's question. "He's okay, but he has these ranches he services and they're struggling with the horses, some of them are trapped, livestock too."

Compassion flooded Riley's face. "What will they do?"

"Neil had this idea of him and me going down there to help, take some horses."

Riley half smiled. "That is a good idea, when do you leave?"

"Thing is Ri, I'd be leaving you alone, still not entirely fixed, and with the kids."

"And Carol," Riley reminded him, "And your mom, and my parents, and cousins, and anyone else I can get in if I need help. Right?"

"But still, I don't know if I should be going." He needed for Riley to make the decision.

"It's a good idea. Go, do your cowboy thing. Come home safe."

Jack cradled Riley's face. It was difficult to forget how,

post-surgery, there had been so much bruising and swelling. He looked so normal. "I love you," he said with as much feeling as he could so that Riley *knew* he meant it.

"I love you too." Jack kissed him, and Riley gripped his shirt so they could kiss one last time, and then he stepped away.

"Pack some stuff." He waved. "I'll tell the kids."

WHEN JACK ARRIVED IN THE KITCHEN WITH A DUFFLE FULL OF jeans, T-shirts and underwear, he found a small procession of children waiting for him, Hayley at the head, holding Max's hand.

He got hugs from everyone, including Max, and finally he was at the door with Riley.

"Looks like you'll have company." Riley gestured out of the open door. Jack looked past him. Neil was there with the truck, and in the same area, Robbie, Vaughn and Liam, all with similar duffels. Robbie and Vaughn were hooking up trailers to the ranch trucks, Liam leading in the first of the ranch quarter horses, workers every one of them.

CHAPTER 6

hey made it to just outside Liberty in five hours, stopping at one of the roads with a view of the river and every man climbed out. Water, and somewhere in there, the river bed, but it had broken its banks and swallowed the land. None of them had seen anything like it. Robbie summed it up the best.

"Fuck."

"Rowdy McGuire's place, my friend Alec is his son." Neil pointed to the left of the main flooding. "Seventy-five head, ten horses, and a house on the edge of the property with some stranded."

Jack got back in the truck. "Then let's go."

Arriving at the McGuire holding was a lesson in how quickly things could turn to shit. The main house itself was dry, built on a slight rise, but the yard and pens were all under at least a few inches of water.

"The water table is fucked." Robbie crouched down to feel the earth beneath the low water. "The earth is sodden, nothing is draining away."

"And we're on a hill here," someone interrupted. "Rowdy

McGuire," he added, and shook hands with Jack and his team. "Think how bad it is on lower ground there." He gazed past Jack to the fields beyond, his lined face a picture of misery. "Two of my guys are down with injuries; I lost three of my workhorses. There's no one to call on, we're overwhelmed."

"Where do you need us to start?" Jack looked up at the sky, there was still a good three hours until twilight and they could at least get the lay of the land.

He turned to Jack. "Twenty head are cut off from the main herd; we've got time today to get them out simply enough with your help."

They looked at each other and Jack's rancher-heart felt Rowdy's pain. They had over fifty other head of cattle out there stuck, not to mention horses. But they had to choose their battles.

Jack settled his Stetson on his head. "Let's get this done."

They saddled up at speed, and left the ranch in the direction of the stranded cattle, the water deepening as they headed downhill. Jack was riding the most dependable workhorse they had at the D, Domino, who didn't hesitate to wade into the water. Rowdy led the way; he knew the ground, knew where the problems would be, like hidden posts, or fencing, but right now the water was only maybe three feet high, enough to brush Jack's boots. They'd all donned wet weather pants but the heat, even this late in the day, was stifling. It was still so freaking hot the compulsion to slip from the horse's back and into the water was a strong one Jack had to ignore.

A rider drew level with him, Rowdy's son and Neil's friend, Alec, "Thanks for this, Mr. Campbell-Hayes."

Jack tipped his hat. There was no need to exchange words; cowboys did what they could to help. It was a code that he lived by. He did have one thing to say though. "Jack," he corrected. "These here are Robbie, Vaughn, and Liam."

Alec nodded at the men, and then reined in a little to retake his place at the rear of the group. He probably knew the ranch as well as his dad, but he'd taken the role of keeping the group together. Like Neil, he had a huge backpack full of medical equipment; Jack imagined they could handle most things thrown at them today.

Rowdy was the one with the rifle.

Sometimes, the only solution was to euthanize. Jack hated that part of being a rancher and he'd only had to face it twice, both when he was a kid, before his dad left, all part of making Jack a man. He tapped the saddle twice, needing some of that luck now.

They saw the cattle when they rounded the next stand of trees, the river water now a good four feet here and steadily flowing sideways. The pull of the flow wasn't enough to unseat anyone, but Domino snorted and shook his head. Jack patted him, reassured him, and talked to him until they settled back into the walk they'd mastered so far.

"Watch here," Rowdy called back, and Jack passed the message back to Vaughn who was behind him. Jack had to work hard to keep Domino on the same path as Rowdy's palomino, his muscles tight with exertion.

The cattle were scared, ten trapped in a space no bigger than fifty square feet. They were huddled right in the middle of the raised ground.

"They said we'd be okay," Rowdy said, his voice cracking, "said the water wouldn't reach this far."

Jack allowed him a few moments to connect to what was happening. Then he asked the question he needed an answer to. "Where do you want us?"

Rowdy snapped out of it, pushed his Stetson harder on

his head, and wiped his face of sweat. "Alec, you go left, we've got right."

Instinctively Jack's guys split to their usual positions, Jack and Vaughn with Rowdy and his other two cowboys.

"We're taking them up, beyond the house."

Even getting the cattle to move out of the foot of water they were in was nearly impossible, getting them to move into deeper water, wading through the wet stuff, needed so much shouting and cajoling that Jack was hoarse by the end of it.

It took two hours to get them heading uphill, away from the deeper flooding, and to the driest areas way beyond the house.

Rowdy's no-nonsense rancher's wife had dinner on, and had made up cots as she could. The ground floor of the house was nearly empty; everything of value had been moved to the top floor just in case.

"Never seen anything like this," Rowdy said again, for the tenth time. This time with food in his belly and a beer smoothing the edges. "They said it wouldn't reach us, and then we watched it climb the hill, knowing that right down there sixty-five remaining head were trapped. And the horses…"

By the time Jack was ready for bed he could have slept as soon as his head hit the pillow. Only he didn't, he took his cell to the porch and called Riley. The reception was crappy, the service unreliable there, but it was enough to touch base.

He didn't want to talk about the details, about the devastation that he had seen, the surreal expanse of lake where there should be fields. He didn't like thinking about what was waiting under the water, snakes, fire ants, worse, and posts, debris carried along by the force of the flood; hated the fact he couldn't see.

Riley's voice was what he needed right now. That soft

tone as he whispered over the sleeping kids, and then louder when he took the call outside.

"I love you. Stay safe," were Riley's last words.

And Jack had one thing to say back, "Always. I love you."

THE NEXT DAY, UP AND OUT WITH ONLY A FEW HOURS' SLEEP, wasn't any better. The rest of the cattle were lower down, already up to their flanks in water. The surface of the flood rippled as it moved, like a living thing, the taller grasses just peeking over and bending at the force of the flood. There was a fence and the herd was up against it, as if it was an anchor for them.

"We hadn't sold a lot of the calves," Rowdy said, grief in his voice. "There's calves, tiny babies, under this, drowned."

They'd talked last night about what the flood would reveal when it subsided, and it broke Jack's heart to think of the animals that couldn't be saved.

And even then, there were longer-term concerns for the cattle; foot rot from standing in water or muddy fields for long periods and the risk of disease from mosquitoes. None of this was good. Water seemed so benign, but this? Jack looked across the space, the water, some tufts of grass and the very top of a fence line. This was a disaster of epic proportions for the ranches in this area.

Between them they moved the cattle, the going was slow, and the impossibility of getting behind some of them was heartbreaking. There was nothing they could do for the three that refused to move, even roped they were slipping and sliding into the mud under the water. Only when the main herd began to swim-walk through deeper water, and then up the hill, did two of the cows left there move. Jack imagined they were the ones with the babies that were lost under the water.

And the hits just kept coming.

It was early afternoon when they managed to get as many as they could to drier ground, and stopped, exhausted, at the main house.

"What's left?" Jack asked, and caught the look between Alec and his dad.

Rowdy shrugged. "Stranded horses," he said.

"The ones at the house?"

They'd talked last night about six horses at a place just outside the floodplain on the river itself. Raised on stilts because of it's proximity to the river, there was room for the horses to huddle on the porch.

These weren't Rowdy's horses, but that didn't matter.

"It's a boat trip, no horses." Jack glanced over at Domino, who was exhausted and being stabled by Rowdy's wife and their youngest daughter.

Jack took his cell phone out and everything else in his pockets and placed it on a table. "I'm in," he said without hesitation.

Robbie, Vaughn and Liam moved to stand next to him.

"I don't much like boats," Robbie murmured, "but trapped horses, show me the way."

What they came across was nothing that Jack could put into words. One of the mares, older and exhausted, after examination, was trapped, her leg through the porch wood. His gut told him there wasn't any hope. She wasn't in any shape to travel, let alone swim to dry ground. But for the others? The house itself was empty; the horses had been here three days. There was no correlation between horses and owner, the horses had just found higher ground.

"They're barely halter broke." Rowdy jumped from the boat to the porch. The nearest horse flattening its ears and snorting. This was clearly the brave one, the horse that was the barricade between the rest of this small group and the outside world.

Rowdy took his time, talked, moved slowly, and managed to slip a halter on the horse in charge of this motley crew. One by one, they covered the horses' eyes so they couldn't see left and right, haltered them, and led them off the porch then down the slope. All except for the trapped horse.

Jack exchanged glances with Rowdy, nodded, and along with Alec they led the horses away, each man up to his chest in the water.

The rifle shot was loud in the eerie silence of the horses and men making their way in the opposite direction to the river and up to the nearest road. Ranching sure wasn't a Disney movie, there were not always happy endings.

Jack didn't think he would ever forget.

CHAPTER 7

*R*iley watched the news, even caught sight of Jack briefly in a video on YouTube about the horse rescue on the porch. They said people died, that the area would take years to recover, that they didn't know what they would find when the waters receded.

The middle of the night was the worst. Watching stories of people with missing family, a wall that had given way under the pressure of the water, crushing a first responder. There had been graphic film of the rescue, the man who was pronounced dead on scene, and Riley watched it all.

Fear was his constant companion. What would life be like without Jack? How would he carry on for the kids?

People must live on after losing family, but how could he?

Jack was coming home, and Riley was as bad as a kid waiting for Christmas. He'd initially decided he was going to wait inside for Jack, but with no kids or nanny in the house it was quiet in there. So, a full hour before Jack said he'd be home, Riley was out on the fence waiting. He wanted to see Jack so badly, and even after only five days Riley had missed him.

When the first truck and trailer arrived Riley's heart sank. It was Robbie and Liam, not Jack. He hid his disappointment and welcomed them back, helped where he could, got shouted at for getting near the horses and that he should watch his neck. By the time the second truck rolled in, Riley was wound tight, and desperate to make sure Jack was okay. He'd exchanged texts and some FaceTime with his exhausted husband, but reception had been awful and the FaceTime had only lasted long enough for Riley to see that Jack was devastated at what he'd seen.

The tension was evidenced in his expression, the way he held himself, and the way he hugged Riley. Always the cowboy, he dealt with the horses first and then everyone split up to go to their respective homes. Riley tugged Jack into the house.

"Have you eaten?"

"We stopped about an hour back."

"Are you hungry?"

Jack yawned. "No, tired is all."

So Riley continued to tug him through the house to their bedroom and shut the door behind them. Jack went to sit on the bed, but Riley stopped him. "Shower, then bed."

"I'm exhausted, I don't want..." Jack scrubbed a hand through his dark hair and yawned again.

"Come on," Riley insisted, and began to undress Jack, one item of clothing at a time, stopping in between each one to comment on a bruise, or a cut. He asked about every mark revealed, and after a while Jack began to answer, talking about razor wire, and snakes, and the horrible screams of trapped animals and how he couldn't even begin to explain what it had looked like.

And Riley listened, stripping at the same time until they were naked and in their walk-in shower. They didn't kiss, or talk. Riley soaped his hands and loved Jack. In every press of his fingers, in every touch, he loved Jack. He held him up when Jack began to falter, cradled his face to look into his eyes, and watched Jack's slow, soft sleepy smile.

Then he dried Jack with the biggest, fluffiest towels he had.

"Some people lost everything," Jack murmured, as Riley encouraged him to sit on the bed.

"We'll help them." Riley helped Jack tug on the boxers they wore in bed. Too many times the kids had jumped on them and they'd made a silent pact long ago not to sleep naked. It was a compromise they agreed on easily.

He settled onto his side, and then encouraged Jack to lay next to him. He pressed a kiss to Jack's smooth back, nosing at one of the larger bruises.

"I love you," he murmured, but Jack was already asleep, his breathing rhythmic, his body pressing against Riley's. The fact he was asleep didn't stop Riley talking though because he had a lot of mess in his head he wanted to get out. Jack would understand that. "I missed you so much, but I'm glad you went, because that's all you, all the time, thinking about others, helping others. If I didn't love you already, then this would only make me love you more."

BEING WOKEN BY AN ELEPHANT TRAMPLING ON YOUR BALLS IS one thing, having two is quite another.

"Pappa, you're home!"

"Pappa, I won a star, look!"

Lexie and Connor were bouncing on Riley's side of the bed, poking at Jack, whose hair had dried hopelessly in cute, dark tufts.

"Shhh, Pappa's asleep," Riley said.

Jack grumbled something and then turned on his back.

"I'm awake," he announced, with a wide yawn. "Who's that jumping all over me?"

"It's Connor and Lexie!" Lexie shouted and bounced some more. Riley curled in on himself, one knee to his balls was enough already.

"I don't know anyone called Lonnor or Cexie?" Jack teased and blinked up at them.

"Connor and Lexie, silly!" Lexie added, still in the same near-shouted tones.

"Oh...Connor and Lexie, I remember you."

"Didja bring us a present?" Lexie asked, even as she kissed Jack's face.

"Pappa wouldn't have had time," Riley began but Jack nodded.

"Yep, you'll have it after dinner."

Lexie pouted, but then her smile flashed. "Connor, we're helping with dinner," she announced, and Connor went with her.

"You know we said one day she'll be President." Jack let his head fall back on the pillow.

"Yeah?"

"Not just of the US you know, the world."

Riley grinned and half rolled over Jack and they kissed enough to reassure each other that Jack was home. Safe. Then it was back to normal, Lexie helping to chop vegetables, Connor playing on his iPad and explaining how the vegetables were all different thicknesses. Max came in, gave Jack a hug and then went under the table with Toby. Hayley arrived with all the drama of someone who was running late, and apologized and hugged and apologized again.

Soon she wouldn't be there to run late at all, she'd be at college doing her thing, and even as Riley watched her smiling and laughing with Jack, his heart hurt. In four weeks it was her birthday and going away party all in one go; a typical Campbell-Hayes celebration with banners, and family, and barbecue.

Tomorrow, Riley and Jack were gift shopping as well as choosing a cake. But what did you choose for a young woman who was leaving home? She was beyond princesses, and teddy bears in jeans. This had to be grown-up, but for the life of him he wasn't feeling the right kind of present for her.

The things that made him worry these days amazed him. Before Jack, before kids, it was all about what people owed him, what was going to be his. Now he was solely focused on family, on what he could give to them. They kept him grounded.

What happened when they all left? Would he just become what he used to be? Was he only a good guy because of them? Would he return to being selfish and self-absorbed?

"Penny for them?" Jack whispered, right in his ear, startling him out of his spiraling thoughts.

"Not worth that," Riley snapped a quick comeback, and then winked. Let Jack think that he was contemplating his ass or something. Anything but the serious stuff that sometimes blindsided him.

"How about a champagne bottle?" the cake guy suggested.

Riley knew he'd introduced himself but he'd not heard properly and was now resigned to thinking of him as the cake guy. "Boring," Riley said. "Sorry, I didn't mean…"

Cake guy waved a hand as if he'd heard it all before. "I know, it's a classic celebration cake for someone off to college but I'm sure we can come up with something better."

"She won't be eating much of it anyway," Jack pointed out. "She's diabetic, but she wouldn't want a low sugar anything."

"Says low sugar stuff tastes like crap," Riley finished.

They did that a lot, finishing each other's sentences, and always looked at each other after and smiled. Today was no different. The smile Jack gave him made the gentle laugh lines around his eyes crinkle and Riley was lost again in their blue depths. He probably had the same kind of lines; they laughed a lot.

All the time.

Well, the times that Riley wasn't angsting over something.

"Riley?"

Riley blinked back to the discussion. "Sorry, what did I miss?"

"Allen was asking about what kinds of things Hayley likes?"

"What did you say already?" Riley asked.

"Horses, geology, her family."

Riley couldn't think of much to add to that, apart from maybe Logan, but he came under family, or at least extended-but-not-by-blood family.

Allen, as Riley now knew he was called, tapped his goatee thoughtfully. Then he pulled his sketch pad to himself and drew a quick something that from this angle looked like an ant hill.

"How about layers?" Allen began quietly, "the geological layers under the ranch, and then the horses, and your house maybe, and then representations of her family?" He sketched more and turned it around. Of course the geology he'd represented with some shaded lines was bad, but hell, Riley could fix that and explain just how the red layer was under the blue and then gray. Or at least tell him what layers of the cake should be what color. Could Allen even make a gray cake?

"I love that idea," Jack said. "Riley, what do you think?"

"I love it, I can help with the geological layers, they have to be right, or she'll know, she's really clever, you know." Riley puffed up with pride at their daughter, and at the fact that she wanted to learn what he loved.

"I can see that." Allen smiled. "My email is in there, if you want to send me the geological information."

"No need." Riley reached out for the sketch pad, which Allen handed over along with the pen. "Do you have colors?" Allen pushed a pot of Sharpies toward Riley and within five minutes Riley had a topographically accurate representation of the rocks that the D sat on. Okay, it might be overkill, but it needed to be right.

Allen took it back and nodded. "We can do this. Now, tell me more about your home and the horses, and of course, your family."

Jack did most of the talking. Riley had moved onto thinking about the gift they wanted to get Hayley, or rather the fact they'd not made any decisions at all.

"Jewelry is always good," Jack said after they'd stood outside the last store on this floor looking for inspiration.

"She doesn't wear a lot of jewelry." Riley poked at the window of the gift shop morosely. Why was it so difficult to find the most perfect present in the history of presents? "And it's what anyone could buy her."

Jack nodded and then his face brightened. "Hang on." He grabbed Riley's hand, pulling him back to the last jewelry store they'd stood outside of. He pointed at the display of bangles, and at one in particular which was a rose gold bracelet they'd both admired. The design was simple, a delicate three-quarter band closed with a chain and a simple knot of the gold to hold the chain together. Nothing too flashy, but very much Hayley.

"How about, because she is going away, we get it engraved with everyone's names, and maybe the longitude and latitude of the ranch? Her home?"

Riley fell in love with Jack all over again and all he could think was that it was perfect.

The assistant helped them, found them an engraver, and three hours later they had the gift wrapped and a card written. They were ready, they had the perfect gift, a card, and Hayley would know they loved her.

Riley just hoped the party was enough for Hayley to take some good memories with her of birthdays and home and family.

CHAPTER 8

"When is Logan getting here?" Hayley asked. She'd been hanging around the barbecue at her going away / birthday party for a while now, shooting the breeze with Jack and Josh, but it had been clear that she was angling to talk to Josh about Logan all along.

"He said he'd be here about seven, sweetheart," Josh said.

She glanced at her watch and then sauntered away as if she hadn't been angling for that information at all.

"Uh oh, is Hayley waiting for Logan?" Josh asked Jack.

"Yeah," Jack said. "She's crushed on him since she first arrived here. Always said she'd marry him one day. Doesn't matter he's your son and is likely a freak—"

Josh thumped him then picked up tongs. "He still asks after her all the time," Josh turned the last of the steaks. "Over and above talking about coming home. I know the two things are separate, we talked about it."

"That's good, thing is Hayley's so far gone on Logan that I'm not sure anyone will ever come up to that."

Josh frowned at Jack "I guess when you know who the one is…"

"Yeah," Jack murmured. "So he's still talking about switching colleges?"

He wasn't sure he should bring the subject up, but it seemed to him that as Logan's uncle it was a reasonable question to ask and Josh had mentioned it first.

"He has a place at UT in Austin, swears he just wants to be closer to home, and tells me he wants to work with me."

"As I said, Campbell and Campbell."

"I still think he has a thing for Hayley."

Jack looked at his brother, wondering if their previous chat wasn't fully done, and Josh still had some thoughts that Logan's decision was her fault. He realized he must be giving a death stare when Josh snorted with laughter. "It's fine, he's a grown man and yeah, I'm excited we could do something together."

Crisis averted, Jack and Josh returned to grilling and he glanced over at Riley who was giving a piggyback ride to Connor and who had a line of children waiting their turn. The big idiot was hot and dusty and grinning like a fool.

Just the way Jack liked him.

When the piggyback ride passed near the barbecue Jack called out to Riley, who jogged over, a laughing Connor gripping at his hair.

"Wassup?" Riley asked, and reached up to loosen Connor's hold.

"I love you." Jack leaned forward for a kiss.

Riley didn't even question Jack's need for contact, and they kissed gently, Connor squealing as Riley bent over. When they parted Jack searched Riley's eyes, and there it was, the spark of passion.

Arousal zipped through Jack's body. "You. Me. Barn. As soon as everyone goes home."

Riley's eyes narrowed, and his tongue darted out to wet

his lips. They may as well have been the only two people at this event.

"Uh huh," Riley said, "I can get on board with that plan. You want to me to tell everyone to leave right now?"

Jack shook his head. "We have to be polite and entertain everyone for a little bit longer," he deadpanned.

Riley gave one of his patented wide smiles. "We'll have to raincheck until later then."

They kissed one more time; Jack ignoring his brother's teasing about gay cooties on the steaks, and a squealing Connor wanting more ride.

"Jack?" Riley asked.

"Hmmm?" Jack hummed into the half-kiss.

"I love you, too."

Jack saw Logan the minute he arrived at the party. Not that he'd been watching for him in particular, even though he knew Hayley was on hot bricks waiting for him to get there. He just happened to be out front of the house manning the barbecue with Josh, as usual, when Logan arrived in the beat-up old truck that he loved so much. He parked and stepped out of the cab, rolling his neck and looking skyward, stretching tall. Jack tried to find Hayley to see if she was here witnessing the arrival of the boy she wanted.

Man. Actually, Logan was a man. He was twenty-two and had done his time in pre-law up in New York with some pretty impressive LSAT scores, or so Josh had told him the day Logan had found out.

He'd be finished with college soon, well at least the first chunk of it, following his dad, into law, so no, he wasn't a boy anymore.

"Logan's here." Jack bumped elbows with Josh who was seasoning steaks and poking at them with a fork.

Josh grinned over at his son, then his mouth fell open. Jack wondered what the hell he'd seen that would cause that reaction of shock.

That was when he saw the blonde climbing out of the truck, tottering around the front on thin heels.

"She's gonna break an ankle," Josh commented.

"And they're both gonna break Hayley's heart," Jack muttered and was pleased when Josh didn't hear him.

"Looks like Logan has a girlfriend," Josh said.

Logan and the blonde talked for a while, hugged, and then she cradled his face before pressing a kiss to his forehead. He offered his arm and she clung to it and then they made their way toward the family under the big awning that provided shade.

"Clearly, he has the Campbell genes." Josh smirked. "We like'm blonde."

Jack wanted to say something but didn't, because Riley was a blond. So Josh was mostly right there. He still couldn't see Hayley, and then she appeared from the house, beautiful in a summer dress, her hair long and loose around her shoulders. She was eighteen but she wore a little makeup and appeared older, and so much like her dad now that it sometimes hurt to look at her. She was Jack's daughter as well; maybe not by blood, but she was his. Had been since she'd arrived, a kid without a mother who just wanted to be loved.

Jack saw the moment Hayley noticed Logan, or at least pretended to notice him. She dead stopped and stared at him and then, drawing her shoulders back, finished the walk to where he stood.

"Hold the fort," Jack said and left Josh with the barbecue. Given he hadn't seen Logan in a while, he guessed Josh would be pissed at not going over straight away, but tough, Hayley needed some moral support when the young man she said she was going to marry turned up at her birthday barbecue with someone else.

Luke beat him to it.

"You okay there, Hayls?" Luke hip-checked her, and she had to catch her balance on the fence. Luke might well have been Riley's nephew and part of the extended Campbell-Hayes' cousin group, but even Jack found his devil-may-care attitude frustrating at times.

In his third year at Yale, he looked so much like Jeff that sometimes just seeing him reminded Jack of everything Luke's asshole of a father had done. Still, Luke wasn't his dad and despite being frustratingly idiotic he had a good heart and watched out for his mom. He was getting to the point where Jack knew that Lisa would want to tell him what had happened with his dad.

One more person who would know the family secret. Jack tried not to worry about that, and concentrated on the here and now.

"I'm fine," she answered Luke's question. Jack stopped a couple of feet to the side of him, ready to… god knows what.

Luke whistled. "Wow, is that Logan's girlfriend? She's hot."

Hayley feigned indifference. "Who?"

Luke pointed a finger in Logan's direction and Hayley rushed to grab his arm and pull it down.

"Don't do that," she snapped.

"Why Hayls, you don't want him knowing you're looking?" He delivered this in an annoying sing-song voice, and she thumped him in the arm hard, and stepped away. "The fuck?" he muttered.

"Go away Luke; you're an idiot."

Jack tended to agree, Luke was one of those boys who just loved to push buttons, but so far Hayley was handling everything okay.

With another grin, Luke swept Hayley up into his arms and held her tightly, carrying her kicking and scratching over to where Logan and his blonde were talking to Eli and Robbie.

Everyone turned to watch when Luke dropped her onto her rump.

"You're an asshole Luke!" she shouted and scrambled to stand, brushing the dust off her butt and then her hands.

Jack was about to move, but Riley was there, and he stopped him, a hand on his arm. "She'll deal with it," he said. He watched from there, and he continued to watch all afternoon when he was manning the barbecue. At one point, she and the blonde disappeared into the house, but there were no cat fights, nor arguing. Just a contrite Logan hanging around the barbecue and chatting with Josh.

"Tell us about your girlfriend." Jack interrupted the heated debate about which football team was best. That was a moot point, the Cowboys were better than anyone else.

"She's not my girlfriend," Logan said, not quite meeting Jack's eyes.

"She's not?" Josh asked, sounding shocked.

"Cassie's a friend. We were at a party last night and somehow she ended up in my car here, so I said she could stay, y'know Southern hospitality and all that."

"It's fine," Jack said. Making a note to tell Hayley that, although Hayley and Cassie had re-emerged from the house. Seemed like Cassie had borrowed some of Hayley's clothes, and looked less party girl and more girl next door. It didn't stop Luke, who was right up in Cassie's space, although Cassie didn't seem that spooked by it. Logan moved away, talking to family, acting like there was nothing he wanted to do more. But Jack saw him looking for Hayley.

All Jack could think was that he was turning into a social commentator for young adults. He'd never seen that one coming, and he had to go through it with another daughter when Lexie got to Hayley's age.

He decided there and then that Lexie wasn't going to get any older. She'd stay the age she was now forever.

"Hey sexy." Riley helped himself to a piece of steak from the warming plate. He made appreciative sounds as he ate and Jack was hard. It was that easy. One sex sound, one smile, one look at Riley and he was all turned on. Thankfully, he'd become so used to it that he'd taken to never tucking his shirt in. Ever. Not even by accident.

"Hey back," he said, and kissed his man, fingers curled into Riley's hair and his grip firm. When they separated after Josh made some comment about a bucket of cold water, Riley was dazed and pressed a finger to his lip.

"What was that?" he asked.

Jack pasted a fake leer on his face. "If you don't know by now…" Then he decided to be completely honest. "Love you."

Riley smiled, and then kissed Jack. "Love you, too. You think that girl with Logan is his girlfriend?" He sounded a little sad, because he probably thought the same as Jack; that Hayley's heart was going to be broken.

"Nope, not his girl, apparently," Josh interrupted. Then with a nod of his head he indicated Cassie and Luke who were standing very close over by the fence. "Anyway, looks like Luke is all over her like a rash on a baby's bum."

Jack had an uneasy feeling about all of this.

CHAPTER 9

*R*iley was determined that he was going to be brave about this whole college thing. He still felt, on occasion, that he'd missed so much of Hayley's life that he needed to see her every day, just so he could catalog every moment and make up for his absence.

"Must be hard to watch Hayley grow up and go to college," Eli said at his side.

And being strong went right out of the window.

Riley gripped his best friend's arm and hauled him around the back of the house. He ignored the concerned look Jack threw his way, the smile Donna threw him as they marched past, and the fact that Eli was wriggling in an attempt to get away. They came to a stop out of view of everyone, and Riley finally released Eli

"I can't do it," Riley blurted as Eli stepped back and away rubbing his arm.

"What?" Eli asked, "And dude, you don't know your own strength."

Riley's fears vanished in an instant when he saw Eli massaging his arm. "Shit, did I hurt you?" Eli was cancer free, but Riley was always sure to be extra careful with Eli; something Eli hated.

"Fuck off with the cancer pity," Eli snapped his usual response and crossed his arms over his chest. "What can't you do?"

Riley's fears poked back at him, sharp and painful. "Deal with Hayley leaving us."

"She isn't though; she'll be in Colorado studying, as a lot of other girls her age."

"Alone."

Eli sighed. "Riley she won't be alone, she'll meet a guy, let's call him Dave, and despite the tattoos and piercings and the motorbike he'll love her, and only let her have the soft drugs."

Riley sighed noisily. "You're not helping."

"Dave will look after her all through the pregnancy."

"Eli, for god's sake. She's…" Riley couldn't even begin to vocalize the entire mess in his head where Hayley was on her own out there in the world without him and Jack backing her up. Not to mention being without all the other guys on this ranch who kept an eye on things when Riley couldn't.

Eli stepped closer and placed a hand on his arm. "She's what, Riley? When I see Hayley, all I see is confidence and this bright love of life that just shines around her. She is loved and loves, and she is the most sensible person I've ever met." Then he snorted a laugh. "She must get that from her mom."

Riley couldn't even rise to the familiar teasing. "What about her diabetes?" He could hear himself clutching at straws like an idiot.

Eli frowned at him. "When was the last time that was a problem?"

"It's not that, but what about her medical checks and—"

"Riley, you need to breathe." Eli shook him a little and

Riley snapped out of it.

"I am breathing," he murmured. "I'm just losing my shit here, and Jack is all calm and keeps saying things like 'It's only Colorado,' and what am I supposed to say to that?"

"Do you remember our first year in college?"

"That's not helping either," Riley groaned and scrubbed at his eyes. "You know what I was like, there are boys out there and all they'll want is to… do things." No boy was going to treat Hayley as he had treated girls in college. He'd only settled down a bit when he'd met Hayley's mom, but he hadn't even treated her as well as he could've. "What if someone like me…look…what if her heart gets broken and we're not there to help?"

Eli hesitated for a moment, and he looked deadly serious. Riley waited for the words where Eli said that everything was going to be okay; words he could maybe believe.

"She'll get her heart broken," he said and Riley tensed. That wasn't what he was expecting. "She'll meet this Dave, and he'll hurt her, and she'll likely hurt him, and there will be tears. She'll even call you and Jack, and you'll want to drive right up there and hug her, and probably hunt down and kill Dave at the same time."

"Dave would be a dead man," Riley growled as an image of a mean, tattooed, welfare-cheating biker landed in his head fully formed.

"That's part of being a dad," Eli teased. "Look, the reason she *can* go to college is because you are here for her, and she knows that she can count on you always."

"I suppose."

"But something else, the biggest bravest thing she'll do is to solve things for herself without her dads."

Everything Eli said was making sense; Riley's anxiety settled a little. Hayley was a good kid, hell, she was a beautiful, confident young woman now.

"Since when did you get so wise?" Riley mused.

Eli shrugged. "Since Robbie and I did all this talking and thinking about what we wanted next. Y'know, children and all that."

Riley held his breath, Eli worried his cancer would be back, and even though Robbie wanted children, he accepted that Eli was nervous. It had been enough just to get Eli to agree to marry him, let alone expand the family.

"And?" Riley asked, needing to focus on something other than his embarrassing meltdown.

"It's big, but we've talked to Marcus; he's a good guy, says he'd help us work our way through it all."

Riley pulled Eli into a close hug. "I'm pleased, this is huge," he said. He didn't just mean the expansion of Eli and Robbie's family to three or more, but this was evidence that Eli had resolved some of the issues in his head around cancer, or at least had come to terms with them.

"Don't go telling anyone except Jack, not until Robbie and I have signed on the dotted line."

Riley mimed zipping his lips and nodded. "Promise."

The tantalizing scent of barbecue drifted their way, and Eli sniffed the air. "Let's get food."

Riley wasn't feeling completely settled, but he listened to Eli, and he knew himself that Hayley would be fine; he was just an overprotective idiot who needed his head examined.

He couldn't see Hayley when he and Eli got back to the barbecue, which was a shame because Riley wanted a hug right at that moment, but he was happy to carry Connor around on his back again pretending to be a horse. He'd find Hayley in a bit.

And he would try his hardest to let her go to college without getting too emotional.

Well, apart from the crying, obviously.

CHAPTER 10

*P*ost-barbecue, there was the huge cake with all its multilayers. Eden had collected it, because there was no way they could have it in the house; it wasn't the kind of thing that fit into a Tupperware container. Singing happy birthday as the evening drew in, and then getting to hug his kids, was heaven as far as Jack was concerned. The cake was a huge success; a towering thing that had the horses and the ranch and the kids, with the surprise layers; Jack hoped that Hayley realized what they were, for Riley's sake. He hadn't needed to worry.

"Drift plain with saucer topography, Paleozoic upper and lower carboniferous, Pleistocene Kansan drift." She pointed at the colors. "This is so cool."

Logan had sidled up to her, half hugged her as she blew out her candles, and Jack couldn't fail to notice she leaned into him a little. Not for long, but enough that it made Jack think that shit was about to hit the fan. What if she told Logan how she felt? Not the 'I'm gonna marry Logan' talk from when she was younger, but this fresh bloom of young romance that Logan could destroy in a single word. It didn't matter that Logan was a good guy, and Jack's nephew, this was Hayley's heart that was on the line here.

"Okay?" Riley said as everyone gathered around for a slice of cake. Jack didn't have to say a word. He inclined his head in the direction of Hayley and Logan sharing a huge slice of ranch and horse on a plate. Logan leaned down and whispered something in her ear, and she smiled and then it happened, Logan walked away and Hayley followed, and suddenly they were out of sight around the corner of Jack and Riley's barn.

Jack wanted to follow, and he could feel Riley's tension as well. He already imagined the division of labor if the shit hit the fan. Riley would console Hayley and Jack would pummel Logan into the ground. Metaphorically of course, after all Logan was his nephew.

When Hayley reappeared, with Logan a few steps behind her, she didn't look as if she was crying, or devastated, or anything of the things Jack had been expecting. She was smiling, and wait…oh shit.

Was Logan holding her hand?

WITH EVERYONE GONE, THE RANCH WAS A DIFFERENT PLACE. The hundreds of small lights were switched off, all except one row that Jack had left on around the front door. He liked their glow, and he could always tell people he wanted them up for the kids. Everything else they would sort in the morning. He closed and locked the door, and came face to face with Riley and Hayley at the table nursing hot chocolates with a plate of cookies between them.

Jack couldn't eat another thing, but in this family, chocolate and cookies were symbolic of a need for a conversation.

"We have a drink for you Pappa," Hayley said.

Jack slid into his seat, opposite Riley and next to Hayley.

Maybe this was where she told them that she was over Logan. Maybe he'd told her that she wasn't his kind of girl, that maybe he wasn't even into girls. Jack didn't know, but he braced himself for the worst.

"So tonight, Logan asked me out," she said, and sipped her chocolate.

"He did?" At least Riley had the power of speech; Jack mostly wrapped his question in an incoherent grunt.

"He said we could meet for coffee, that he'd come and visit me in Denver."

"What did you say?"

"Yes, of course. I thought when he arrived with Cassie that she was his girlfriend, and it made me feel sad, and angry that I'd never had the chance to show him me, grown-up me I mean. But she's just a friend, and they'd come straight from a party and she borrowed some of my stuff." Hayley leaned forward, "I found her and Luke out by the stables kissing," she said, conspiratorially. Then she leaned back, "anyway, Logan didn't kiss *me* or anything, but I like him and I wanted to let you know."

She was obviously waiting for them to make a comment. Jack was at a loss. What they wanted for her was a guy with a purpose, who looked after her, who came from a family that respected the concept of family as much as they did, someone who made Hayley smile.

He was going to let Riley have this one, let him say what they thought, but Riley was silent and was looking at *him*. Wait? What? Riley gave him a look, that one which said, *she's your daughter too.*

"I like Logan," he said, and then coughed. "I love Logan, of course I would, he's my nephew, and he's grown up, and..." He flailed for anything else to say that didn't sound really weird. "I hope you have fun," he added lamely. Riley raised an eyebrow, and clearly Jack hadn't done so well on the awkward conversation front.

"We want you to be happy," Riley began. Oh this should be good; Riley was not going to be happy about this at all. Not that it was to do with Logan specifically; just any boy anywhere near Hayley. "And I think Logan has always made you happy, and sometimes…" He reached over and grasped Jack's hand. "…you just know, you feel it's right. I hope, no, *we hope*, that you have fun on the date, and that Logan is aware your Pappa has a shotgun."

Jack couldn't help the snort of laughter that escaped him. Logan was very aware of what was in the gun cabinet.

"So when are you meeting?"

"He said he'd come up to see me in a couple of weeks." Her cell vibrated and her face lit up. "It's him." She pushed up from the table. She kissed Jack's cheek and hugged him, and then it was Riley's turn. With a wave and a smile she headed for bed.

Alone in the kitchen the two men stared at each other.

"Logan," Riley said.

"Yep," Jack replied.

"She always said…"

"Yep, she did."

They sat in silence for a moment. The house was quiet, the twins and Max in bed, Carol asleep, Hayley in her room.

"You remember what you said…" Riley began.

Oh Jack remembered exactly what he said, and fuck, now that Riley was on the same page they needed to get out there now.

The Barn. Their place.

CHAPTER 11

*R*iley was determined that this time he would be the one taking care of Jack. That was from the minute the door shut on them and Riley locked it. They kissed, but when Jack pressed him back against the door he switched their places in a smooth move and had the upper hand. Jack made a show of reversing the hold, but his lips were parted and his cock hard and Riley knew this was all on him now.

The first thing he did, because he needed a taste of Jack right now, was to drop to his knees onto the blankets that were there for this purpose, and nuzzled Jack's groin. He smelled of denim, barbecue smoke, and Jack and Riley didn't hesitate to unbutton the fly of Jack's best jeans. He pulled the pants enough to get to Jack's boxers, and slipped them down just below Jack's balls, and he finally had what he wanted. For a moment he stared, because he wanted to savor this part where he knew Jack would move, and maybe beg, or at least moan in need.

"C'mon," Jack whispered, and moved against Riley, and that was what Riley'd been waiting for. He chuckled and pressed his face to Jack's cock, his tongue tracing a pattern on the soft skin. Jack groaned, that was the last hint Riley was getting, and he was happy to go with it.

He licked and sucked and Jack didn't move an inch. That was the deal, Jack wouldn't move until Riley said he could; the power was incredible and Riley was so hard in his pants it hurt. He adjusted himself, loosening his jeans, until his own erection was free, and with one hand slipping the length of it, he went to town on Jack's cock. There wasn't an inch of it that wasn't worshipped, and when Jack's thighs strained and his breathing sped up, that was it, Riley pulled off. He didn't want to miss Jack coming with Riley's cock in his ass, and that wasn't going to happen if Jack finished now.

Riley used Jack to stand and for a while they kissed, Riley taking care not to grind against Jack, because fuck, he really wanted to have his husband bent over and... he couldn't even think about it.

"There." He nodded toward one of the corners where Jack had left a table. He'd sanded it smooth, it was just the right height and as they crossed to it, Jack removing his boots, jeans and boxers, Riley grabbed the lube from its hiding place.

Jack leaned over the table, spread his legs a little and Riley stared... at the toned skin, strong thighs, at Jack's ass, which was gorgeous, and at Jack looking back at him with one raised eyebrow. In seconds he was stripped, completely naked, and he yanked at Jack's shirt and T-shirt until they were off as well. He just wanted all that flesh available to mark with his teeth and hands. He couldn't resist smacking Jack's bare ass, and Jack didn't complain, just pushed his ass out against the crack of Riley's palm. The handprint was faint, but his skin pinked, and Riley did it again. He cataloged the way Jack tensed, and the delicious sound of Jack's groan, and ran a hand over the warmth he was creating there. Riley squeezed lube onto the base of Jack's spine and then smoothed it down to Jack's ass, cracking his hand one last time on Jack's other cheek and at the same time rubbing his hole.

"Riley, fuck."

Riley pressed his finger inside, kissing Jack's spine, adding more lube and pressing down on Jack's shoulder so he was flat on the table.

"You're beautiful." He ran a hand from shoulder to ass cheek where it was still warm. "I'm going to fuck you so hard."

Jack moaned and pushed back on Riley's finger, so Riley added another, and then he couldn't wait any longer, slicking his cock and holding Jack still.

"I love you," Riley said, his voice cracking, as he paused until Jack could take him inside, and then he was in, and Jack writhed, and Riley held him.

"Riley, harder, fuck me harder."

Riley set up a punishing rhythm, and watched Jack grip the corners of the table. This angle was perfect, he was so deep, but he worried Jack's thighs would mark against the wood, and then he knew he wanted that, and he didn't pull out and, fuck, Jack wasn't moving back.

"Am I hurting you?" Riley managed.

"Harder," was Jack's only reply.

"I'm close," Riley said, and then he was fucking his way inside and coming so hard he shut his eyes and shouted Jack's name. Without ceremony he pulled out, turned Jack and pushed him back on the table, pulling him forward a little, gripping his scarlet ass cheeks and swallowing him down. Jack scrabbled for balance and then lost it, coming hard up Riley's throat, whimpering and unsteady and gripping Riley's hair tight.

"I love you," he said as the last tremors left his body, and

Riley helped him up. Funny how seeing your lover, your husband, unsteady on his legs, made you feel a million kinds of powerful and smug. Which lasted until he saw Jack wince, and then he felt guilty.

"Did I hurt you?" he asked urgently.

Jack chuckled. "I'll feel you for days," he hooked his hands around Riley's neck, "and no, you didn't hurt me."

They kissed deeply, as if it was the punctuation to what they'd just done, coming off the high, and just being together. When they parted Jack smiled at him. "That was intense," he murmured.

Riley should have apologized, or gloated, or felt weird, or something, but he didn't. Because, fuck, that had been intense, so instead he used two simple words. "I know."

Back in their bed they slept like the dead right through the night, but when Riley woke he was still twisted up with Jack, wrapped in his arms, and caged by his legs.

And it was the best morning wake-up, ever.

SHOWERED AND DRESSED AND HAVING KISSED JACK thoroughly, Riley made his way to the kitchen and was surprised to see Eli sitting at the table watching *Toy Story* with Max. Carol was cooking breakfast and the twins were ready for school and waiting for Robbie to drive them as he'd promised he would.

"Morning," Riley said, "You okay?" he always asked that whenever he saw Eli, couldn't help himself, and expected Eli to come back with some quip in his defense, but this morning he was serious.

"I'm great," he said, but he didn't sound great, he sounded nervous.

Riley's chest tightened and he felt the world stop. In a haze, through Robbie picking up the kids, to Carol taking

Max for school. Was this the news they never hoped to have? That Eli was ill again? Eli looked shocked, but Robbie acted pretty normally this morning. He kissed Eli as he left with the twins, nothing out of the ordinary.

Riley put off the inevitable as long as he could, making him and Eli coffee and hesitating to sit down.

"These came yesterday." Eli slid an envelope to Riley.

All Riley could think was, this has to be bad news.

I don't want to read the letter. Please don't make me see the letter.

Eli continued, "And I don't know what to do."

"Shit, Eli…"

"They're only eight and six, but still that's old enough to have seen so much, and what if we're not like you and Jack, what if we can't do this? What if it's wrong for us to think we can even do this?"

Riley blinked at Eli, and then checked out the paperwork, and abruptly everything made sense. This wasn't a scare, this wasn't Eli relapsing, or coming out of remission, or anything like that. This was the adoption at its final stages. Little Louise and Jeremy, parents killed in some weird murder-suicide pact, had been matched to Eli and this must be the letter that confirmed that, finally, Louise and Jeremy would be moving to Eli and Robbie's place. On the ranch. Here. Which meant they had a support network of people who could help.

"It's like pre-wedding nerves," Riley said, and hoped Eli understood what he was trying to say. Eli shook his head, so nope, Riley was talking out of his ass.

He continued, "I remember the day you started this process, I remember witnessing the signing of the forms, the talking to the counselors, and your doctors, it's been nearly a year and it's taken every moment of your time, and now suddenly, it's done. It's like the night before you're getting married—you've spent so long planning the wedding that you've forgotten the reason you're getting married.

Eli's eyes widened, as if maybe some of what Riley was saying was actually making sense. Jack was so much better at this sort of thing than he was; Riley used analogies that got muddled and sometimes made things worse.

"What if I can't do this—?"

"You can do this."

"And what if I get ill—?"

"You won't."

"And what—?"

"Eli, stop! You can sit there all you want looking at all the worst possibilities, but these kids need a stable family, a network of people. They need wide open spaces, and horses, and friends, and you can give them that. You have a heart full of love and you'll be a great dad."

"You think?" Eli was pale.

"What did Robbie say?"

"He hasn't seen this yet, if I show him it will be real."

Riley reached over and cuffed Eli upside the head. "Idiot," he said with affection.

"Okay," Eli said, and breathed slowly and deeply. "I can do this."

Then he smiled and normal I-can-defeat-it-all Eli was back, and with it his sense of humor. "Did you really just say I had a heart full of love?"

Riley huffed a laugh, "Bite me."

Eli stood and Riley hugged him for a long time. The door opened and Robbie coughed to clear his throat.

"You macking on my man, Riley?" he asked wryly.

Riley released his friend, hugged a surprised Robbie and then let them have the kitchen in peace.

He needed to find Jack, not to tell him because that was

Robbie's news to tell, but just to hold him close and tell him that the world was a wonderful place and that he loved him.

Oh, and yeah, to tell him the news as well.

Obviously he wouldn't be able to keep it inside. Jack would just have to act surprised when Robbie told him.

The amount of secrets Riley had told Jack? Well, Jack was a good actor now.

This wouldn't be the first time.

LOUISE AND JEREMY HAD VISITED THE RANCH BEFORE, THEY both knew Riley, and they loved Jack and his horses, but this time it was different. They were moving here permanently and Louise was incredibly protective of her brother. The siblings held hands a lot and looked at each other when one was asked a question. The start in life they'd had was one that Riley wouldn't have wished on any child.

Robbie and Eli had built an addition to their house, two bedrooms, both with big beds and a shared bathroom. Robbie had been the one to suggest the big beds, because the children liked to sleep together; were probably used to it. They'd decorated them both neutrally, and along with Hayley's help they'd filled closets with clothes and toys. None of it was on show, there was no trying to buy affection involved.

All apart from the ponies, of course.

Robbie said every child should have a pony, qualifying it with the extra, every child whose parent worked with horses on a ranch and had the money and access should have a pony. Eli let him have that one thing.

Riley visited briefly, with Connor and Lexie, but Louise held back a little even when Jeremy joined in the impromptu game of tag in the yard. She was watchful and careful and Riley's heart broke for her.

The ponies were what broke the impasse. As horses do, they were unashamedly demanding of treats and nuzzles and as Connor and Lexie showed the two newcomers how to do this or that, or what to touch, and what to say, Louise began to relax.

By the time Riley left, with a grateful glance from Eli, Louise was reading to Jeremy on the sofa, and leaning against Robbie.

This little family would be great, would be the best for each other, and Riley hugged Eli on the way out. He couldn't have wished for a better ending for his friend.

And carefully, and slowly, the families who called the D their home grew by another two.

CHAPTER 12

"Colorado isn't that far," Jack said for the fifth time that week as the days counted down to Hayley leaving. Riley didn't know who was Jack trying to convince; Riley or himself. "Not much more than an hour by plane," he added.

"Uh huh," Riley said, because he'd lost the ability to talk about Hayley and college at the very moment she'd made her final decision on what college she would be attending. Once he'd gotten over the pride that she wanted to learn what he loved, that geology was her choice, it then fell on him just how much her leaving meant to him.

During the rehabilitation on his neck, and when Jack was home from Houston and the floods, there were moments he could forget she was leaving. Times when all six of them sat at the table, or under the table, where Max was concerned, and everything was just peaceful and right.

He and Jack couldn't have been prouder of their daughter, but it didn't stop either of them fretting and worrying.

"I know, but it's not UT, it's not somewhere she can come home anytime she wants to." Riley had become fixated on the idea that there *were* colleges a lot closer than Denver, even though he knew Denver was the best place for everything Hayley wanted.

Jack sighed. "Seriously? Do we really want her to compromise and not go to the college she wanted?"

"Of course not," Riley said. Jack was making sense, as usual. An uncharitable thought crossed Riley's mind that maybe when the twins were ready for college then Jack wouldn't be so calm, and as soon as the idea arrived fully formed into his thoughts, the air left his lungs and he sat down.

Hayley was *their* daughter, the twins were *theirs*. Whatever biology was involved in creating them. Abruptly he wanted to apologize to Jack, to Hayley, hell, to the twins, but Jack crouched between his legs, his hands on Riley's knees.

"I'm going to miss her so much," Jack said, his voice gruff with emotion. "You know that, right?"

Riley nodded, placed his hands on Jack's and they laced fingers. Now it was Riley's turn to reassure Jack.

"It will be okay."

Jack smiled at him. "You could always buy her a jet."

Riley considered the thought for a moment, he had the money, and they could… It hit him that Jack was only teasing and that Riley was an idiot. Hayley might possibly need a car, but not something new, or so they'd been told quite categorically. She didn't want to stand out, and Riley could understand that now.

Way back, before Jack, he'd happily flash his cash, be the big man, drink a thousand-dollar bottle of champagne and spill it everywhere. Now, value was something he put in family and love, not in money. Jack must have seen each individual emotion pass over his face and he waited for Riley to talk.

"Well, shit," Riley finally said.

Jack nodded. "Yeah, that."

They continued putting away clothes and tidying up the desk area; their chore this morning. Jack had left books on the side of the desk, Riley never really did pick up clothes properly, and when Riley had tripped over his own discarded pants last night they were determined to make their room less dorm room and more of a space belonging to responsible adults.

"Dad? Pappa? May I ask something?" Hayley said from behind them.

They turned and she was in the doorway to their bedroom. She was dressed in jeans and a plain T-shirt, with her long blonde hair pulled back into a ponytail. Riley could easily see the little girl who had landed on their doorsteps all those years ago. She didn't seem upset, as if she'd overheard their parental breakdowns over her leaving, so that was one thing.

"What's up?" Jack asked as he stood from piling books in what he deemed a useful and appropriate corner to pile books, and brushed at his jeans.

"Will you make sure that Max is there when I FaceTime from college?"

Riley nodded, although getting Max to interact with some nebulous talking picture of his big sister was always going to be hard. Last time they'd tried it, Max had run screaming from the room, flailing past Connor who ended up on his butt on the floor. "We can try," he said.

Hayley appeared thoughtful. "I think if we do it every time then he'd get used to it."

"We promise to try," Jack interjected.

"And Connor, if he forgives me?"

"And Connor," Riley said, "and he'll be fine as soon as a couple of days have passed."

Although Riley wasn't sure that it would be quite that

quick. Connor was all over the place at the moment. It seemed like his seven-year-old brain was firmly fixed on the concept of Hayley leaving and never coming back. Lexie was much more pragmatic, explaining with all her vast superiority that Connor was stupid. That was an interesting fight that Riley had happened upon; ending up with both twins crying in his arms and him trying not to lose it himself.

"Keep telling them I'll be back for Christmas," Hayley said, the almost permanent worry on her face making Riley's heart hurt. She should be going to college thinking her parents had everything in order and that her siblings understood what was happening.

"We're failing as parents," Riley half-whispered after Hayley had gone.

Jack finished buttoning his shirt and frowned at Riley. "How so?"

"I remember when I went to college I didn't have anything to worry about except maybe leaving Eden, but even then she was balls to the wall and didn't take crap from the family."

Jack cradled Riley's face, and for the longest time, Riley stared into his husband's blue eyes. He could get lost in those eyes, lose himself forever in the promises they held.

"Riley, you weren't leaving a loving home, you were leaving hate and violence and age-old family secrets that made the environment toxic. Of course you didn't care about leaving because you were running away." He pressed a kiss to Riley's lips, and Riley gripped Jack's dark shirt. "On the other hand, Hayley is leaving a family that loves her, that lives together with laughter and all the sweet stuff in life. She'll be sad to leave because between all of us we've made a life here that is kinda impossible to leave even for a day."

"We haven't failed then," Riley murmured. The explanation made sense, but he was still worried. "We want her to be strong and confident, don't we?"

Jack chuckled, and this time the kiss was deeper and way more thorough. Enough so Riley was hard in an instant and contemplating exactly how to get Jack horizontal. Or vertical. Or whatever. Only they couldn't.

"She is strong." Jack eased away. "She's half of you and all of her own woman."

ONE MORE KISS AND JACK LEFT THE ROOM, AND RILEY STOOD still where he was, staring right at the wall of photos that charted the years he and Jack had been together. He felt a tug on his pants and looked down into Max's earnest gaze.

"Hey, Max," he said, and sat next to him when Max scrambled onto his bed. They were closer to each other, Max rambling about something to do with the color red and inspiration hit Riley. Without spooking his son, he reached over to his iPad and laid it on his lap.

"There's red in here," he said.

Max tilted his head and stopped talking, peering curiously at Riley.

Slowly Riley opened the iPad and searched for strawberries.

"Look," he said. "Red strawberries."

Max traced the image with his fingers, not quite touching the screen, hovering above. "Red," he said. His language skills were improving, and he saw a language therapist twice a week at the school he attended, but he still answered with single words, or sometimes by repeating a whole scene from the script of his current favorite—the *Toy Story* films. He stimmed with his hands, flapping them a little and staring at the screen. "Another stunt like that, cowboy, you going to get us killed," he said, still flapping, "Don't tell me what to do!" he added. Of course Riley had no idea of the relevance of that particular line from the films, or the fact that Max repeated it all twice, but he did what he thought was best.

"I know." He nodded, and soothed his son with soft strokes of his hand, until the flapping stopped, and the repeated lines became a wrinkle of his nose and a soft huff.

"Hayley will talk to you in there," he added, but that wasn't a sentence that Max was listening to at all.

"Hey little man," Hayley said from the door, "I was looking for you. Want to go see the horses?"

Max scrambled down; Hayley and Max were so close; he wouldn't understand where she'd gone when she wasn't there at night for him. He already freaked when she couldn't read him a bedtime story. Maybe they should never have got into that routine in the first place. Then, maybe, he would understand, and he might even be able to understand that Hayley was talking to him on the iPad. Riley never knew what he was thinking. No one did, not really.

"Are you coming out with us?" Hayley asked Riley.

"I'll be with you in five," he replied, watching her walk away, Max's hand in hers.

How was he going to do this? How was he going to handle their beautiful, confident, brilliant daughter, leaving for college?

When he walked out into the kitchen he could see Hayley and Max at the fence looking at the horses, Lexie swinging on a gate, and focused, studious Connor reading a book at the table.

Riley had to be the strong one here.

Tomorrow was a big day for Hayley and he could do this.

Right?

JACK WAS DRIVING, WHICH GAVE RILEY WAY TOO MUCH

thinking time, but as Jack knew how he would be, he cranked up some music and the three of them sang along. Hayley was excited, and nervous, and then excited again. She'd cried when they parted, but within half an hour she'd channeled Jack and was showing a brave face to her parents. She couldn't do anything about Connor not wanting to let go of her hand, or Lexie pouting at her brother, or Max stimming, neither could Riley and Jack.

"Being old enough to go to college sucks," she said, and then didn't say anything else. In fact by the time they stopped overnight in Amarillo all three were quiet. Riley had booked a suite at a hotel, and they played cards, watched TV, and had an early night.

The rest of the journey was filled with music and stories, and Hayley's hopes for the future. She wanted an office next to Riley's, she wanted plenty of floor space to spread maps out. She wanted to live at home and maybe they could build a place on the D for her... On and on it went, including a ten-minute discussion on how Logan was so cool, and she couldn't wait to meet up with him.

The talking stopped when the GPS showed they would reach their destination in only twenty minutes.

The rest passed in a complete blur.

They found her dorm room, helped her unpack, and Riley fretted she had to share with someone they didn't know. When they met Skye though, a redhead with a wide grin, she instantly won a place in Riley's heart. She hugged Hayley and introduced them all to her parents who shook Riley's and Jack's hands and made no comments about the fact Hayley had two dads. Maybe it wasn't something Riley needed to worry about, but sue him, he'd worried she'd be bullied or something for the fact that Riley and Jack were her parents.

They'd already visited for orientation in the Summer, but

they'd flown up, and it hadn't seemed real. This here, helping her hang up clothes and make her bed? That was real.

They explored the campus and located the halls, rooms and labs, for her classes, found out where she'd eat and Riley had a debate with Jack over how much did a person need per day to cover food. His concept of just giving her a platinum card made Jack laugh and Hayley frown.

The damned girl was determined to get a job and be independent.

I should be proud. Right?

The building that blew Riley away was the library; yes they had seen it on the tour in the summer, but now, they had the chance to explore and the geological sciences section was huge.

And then, before Riley knew it, with a final hug and kiss they were leaving Denver and heading south.

Home.

CHAPTER 13

*J*ack managed to handle the whole day without losing his cool.

They stopped back at the same hotel in Amarillo, only this time there was no need for a suite. Hayley had already texted them over twenty times, with cryptic messages about her new best friend Skye, and the cute boys on her floor, and how none of them measured up to Logan, and how, to her horror, some of her floor mates had never ridden a horse. The rancher in Jack wanted to bring them all down to the D just so they could all get to ride a horse, and he could imagine Riley chartering a plane.

Yeah, that wasn't happening. Leaving Hayley had been hard, but she was already talking up a storm with Skye, and seemed okay. When they'd said goodbye she had cried, but there had been nothing in the way she'd hugged them that made Jack think that picking her up and putting her back in the truck was a good idea.

They ate in the restaurant, both subdued, but at least they'd talked, and it was probably exactly what Riley needed, because he'd been so quiet in the car.

"I think she'll love college," Jack said, because saying it out loud meant it was true.

"I enjoyed it," Riley admitted.

"I never even wanted to go to college," Jack said, "always wanted my horses, and the ranch."

"I just wanted to drink, and fuck around. Anything to feel good. As you said, college was an escape for me."

Jack had never really pushed Riley about what had things been like back then. Particularly as he'd been right there at Riley's side during the death throes of the Hayes family as it had stood. It occurred to him that he'd never asked about the times when Riley did go home.

"What about the holidays? Was it that bad that you didn't want to go home?"

"I always wanted to come back at Christmas, or summer, and expected things to have changed somehow. Not Eden, she never changed, always smiling, except when Jeff was around. I liked being back, because Jeff never intimidated me and I would get in between him and her, but coming back to Eden who was so lost even though she tried hard to pretend she wasn't? Yeah that was hard sometimes."

He didn't know how they'd got onto the subject of Riley's childhood, but Riley was happy to talk and that didn't always happen where the Hayes family history was concerned.

Then Riley said something that didn't make sense at first, particularly as he was determinedly staring down at his plate as he talked.

"Sometimes when we stand at the fence in the morning, with coffee, or when you're kissing me, or the kids make me laugh, I feel as if I am on the outside looking in."

Pain collected inside Jack from all the dark places he hid it. Did Riley really feel disassociated from their family?

"Riley?"

"I don't mean that I don't think it's happening to me."

Riley began, then sighed, laid down his cutlery and scrubbed at his eyes. "I'm not making any fucking sense."

"Start from the beginning." That was what his mom always said when his thoughts were all tangled, Donna Campbell was a wise woman.

"I deserve good things, and I know that being with you... I couldn't imagine a life without you... but sometimes I'm this twenty-year-old, with hate and fire in his belly and I'm watching this older man with you and I'm surprised at the man I've become."

The pain melted away and instead Jack realized exactly what Riley was saying.

"Eleven years." He reached over and gripped his hand. "We've been together eleven years, we've both changed, and it's all good changes."

"I love you," Riley murmured.

Back inside their room, Jack pulled him into a hug. "I'll never love anyone as much as I love you," he said. He spoke with completely honesty.

Riley gripped Jack's arms, kissed him hard and deep, and proceeded to show Jack exactly how much he loved him back.

———

THEY WERE WOKEN UP BY A TEXT FROM HAYLEY, AND JACK scrambled for the phone at the same time as Riley.

"Is she okay?" Jack asked, urgently.

Riley turned the phone around. "The bacon isn't crispy enough in the canteen," he announced.

Packing and leaving the hotel was difficult when neither of them could stop laughing.

They made it home before dark, and Jack felt immediately at peace as soon as they turned onto the long road that led to the D ranch house. The minute they parked Connor and Lexie were at the car, Max sitting on the doorstep. Behind him Carol looked serious, and shook her head a little to warn Riley and Jack.

Then Connor burst out crying, Lexie joined in, and Max slipped back into the house as fast as he could.

"Lex said she's not coming home forever," Connor said between sobs. Riley had Connor, Jack crouched down by Lexie.

"I didn't say that," Lexie denied, "I said she's not coming back until Christmas, and that it's forever."

Connor sobbed louder. "I love Hayley, I don't want her to go away." He wriggled hard and Riley overbalanced and fell on his ass with Connor curled into his arms. Oh well, that seemed like a good idea. He sat on the ground and pulled Lexie in for a hug.

"Lexie, Christmas isn't forever," Riley began, but that just made Connor hide his face in Riley's arms. Riley sent a despairing look to Jack, as if he wanted Jack to make everything better. It didn't matter that all of a sudden Jack wanted to sit and bawl himself, in the middle of the front yard, right where anyone could see them.

"How long is Christmas?" Connor asked. Jack did some quick mental math multiplying, taking off, dividing and then hoping for the best. He knew better than to give exact counts to any of the kids, but at this moment it was important.

"One hundred and twenty-five days," he said, because that sounded about right. *Was it right? Seventeen weeks...seven days... add a few more.*

Lexie tugged herself free from Jack's grasp, suddenly determined.

"Come on Con, we're making a chart for all the days so we can tick them off."

She pulled at Connor, who was really uncertain, and then

when she sighed and tugged again, he followed, albeit dejectedly.

Riley looked at him and shook his head. "Jack, you gave them days, actual days, you know they'll show Max and if Hayley doesn't come home then…do you not remember the debacle of last Halloween?"

Jack covered his eyes. The last time they'd set numbers of days, something that Max lived by, and that Connor and Lexie cajoled by, was for Halloween and it had been Riley's turn to fuck up the numbers. His number of days was off by two and the entire ranch had to play along that Halloween was actually the 29th of October.

And then Lexie demanded a second Halloween, and sulked for an entire hour when she didn't get it.

Way too much angst.

Jack flopped back on the dirt and Riley leaned over to kiss him before collapsing on top of him.

They lay like that for a while, but it was Riley who was the sensible one.

"Now we need to find Max and explain everything to him."

"And then," Jack said ruefully, "make sure Hayley is definitely back in one hundred and twenty-five days."

Riley rolled to stand and extended his hand, and they stole a quick kiss before going in.

"I'll get cookies," Riley said.

"I'll do the coffee."

Together, with coffee, cookies, and love, they could handle it all.

CHAPTER 14

*R*iley finished his call with Hayley. Two years into her degree now, she was thriving, and she'd asked if there was room to intern at CH. He made a note to ask Kathy, his PA, as soon as he was in. Of course there would be room, hell, he'd make room. But Kathy was the goddess of scheduling, so he'd leave it to her. Riley had only just made it through the door of CH when he was caught by Kathy, and he didn't even have a chance to ask before his morning was ruined.

"You have an online meeting at two with BOEM," Kathy announced, without introduction.

What did the Bureau of Ocean Energy Management want him for today? He thought the next meeting, scheduled for next week would be soon enough.

Riley sighed noisily; it was tradition to appear as pissed off as possible with anything Kathy organized for him even if he didn't mean it. He'd be lost without her and she knew it. She raised a single eyebrow and quirked a smile.

"Can't Tom take it?" He wheedled, that was also a thing he did every time, trying to get Tom to cover the boring meetings that sent him to sleep. All Riley wanted to do was sit with his maps and plan work projects. "What's the point of having a manager if he can't deal with bureaucracy and ticking boxes?"

Kathy just looked at him pointedly. He grumbled a bit more, because that was what he did best. But, with coffee in hand he perched on the side of Kathy's desk, nudging aside a framed picture of her grandchildren so he could get his ass far enough on it. She tutted, and moved the frame to the safety of the other side. From there he could see the picture, her holding two babies, a toddler cuddling her from behind. That could be him and Jack one day, their kids might wait a long time to have children, but one day...

"What?" Kathy asked again with a barely concealed smile.

"Nothing," he lied. Riley tried for innocent but it didn't work; Kathy had been with him too long now to fall for any kind of manipulation. "I was just here to ask how you were."

"I'm fine and no I won't ask Tom to call in to cover a meeting with BOEM. They want to speak to the Hayes in CH Consulting. Do you want to know what things I *have* found out?"

"First, what did they say they want?" A phone call with BOEM wasn't a bad thing, he had a good working relationship with the bureau and was working closely with them on offshore ocean energy capture. He just didn't need it today because he had new maps to look at, and that was what he liked doing.

Best case scenario, it would be a list of questions raised by hurricane activity in the Gulf of Mexico, worst, it could be a serious environmental issue that meant any work Riley and Tom had done was invalid.

"They didn't say." Kathy pulled her pad over. "Tom is down there working on site at the moment. There's nothing that's come up on the radar for complications, and I did a social media search to assess any possible issues. No pressure groups have made themselves known on anything we're working on, the only thing I found was one possible issue with a tract of land that Josiah Harrold and Santone Corp are working. It's five miles inland, oil, and there is some pressure at the state level to go for the quicker, cheaper option to support energy consumption.

"Fuck," Riley cursed. "What the hell are Santone doing down there?"

Santone was the bane of Riley's life. Ethics went out the window as soon as Josiah and his idiot son JJ got involved.

"I can't find anything concrete on that yet, just rumors."

"How does it impact us?" he asked, knowing Kathy wouldn't have brought this up unless she felt there was something that might affect CH.

"It's only a hunch, but I did some research, put in a few calls, and the word is that Santone is looking at a tract of land next to ours, the one Tom is working on. Possibly even wave energy."

Riley's chest tightened. This wouldn't be the first time that Santone sniffed after one of the areas that CH was working on. It seemed like the Harrold family were more interested in working off CH research than their own.

They'd lost Tom a few years back to Riley, and it had hurt them. In Riley's opinion they should have looked after Tom better; Tom had worked for them for a few years as a researcher until JJ, the younger Harrold, had made a pass at him and got a broken nose in return. Tom was small, but he was a scrappy fucker who'd walked away from Santone. Thank God Kathy had found him, because he was as good as Riley, and between them they were finding new and ethical ways to locate energy sources. Something Kathy said clicked abruptly.

"Since when did Santone have any interest in wave energy?"

She shrugged and he didn't really need an answer; Santone saw what CH was doing and they wanted some of Riley and Tom's magic, or luck, or whatever Kathy kept calling it.

"Can you get Tom on the phone?"

He should really go into his office, but out here in Kathy's domain he felt way more comfortable than in his glass room with its city views. In there he felt old school; out here, perched on a desk, he was inspired by the energy from the interns and staff he could see beyond Kathy's glass. He'd much rather have that view.

Kathy pressed speed dial and Tom answered immediately. Riley didn't wait for niceties.

"Santone is sniffing around your site, or as close as dammit."

Tom cursed and then there was the noise of him moving, the shutting of a door and his voice began to echo.

"Riley, this is getting old real quick," he said. "What the hell are they doing?"

"Following our every move it seems, just wanted to give you a heads up. Try not to break JJ's nose again, yeah?"

Tom huffed a soft laugh, but went right back to being serious. "It's a quicker, cheaper alternative without the sustainability. The state infrastructure budget was seriously dented with the work on the dam upstate and the hurricane."

"We have to convince them that our option is the best one."

Riley, or rather CH, had a lot of money riding on this, the investment in purchasing rights had been lengthy and costly. But he was committed to finding ways to power this country without damaging the environment.

"You realize Riley that one day we'll lose, and Santone

will pick up what's left over, that is what they're doing and this is fucking me off, freaking vultures."

"Then we need to make sure we don't lose, because they will go in all guns blazing ripping oil from under the parcel of land instead of working with the State for the wave energy collection."

"Preaching to the choir, boss."

Riley considered the implications of losing momentum when everything had been going so well in the few seconds it took to sip his coffee. Not in detail of course, but enough for his chest to remain tight and his brain to feel all twisted and full of concern. The exposure here was more than CH could handle alone; he'd underwritten a huge amount of the funds personally in a long, convoluted way that only his finance manager truly understood. This falling through would mean a loss to CH, but it would hit him as well. Not enough to destroy him, but enough to hurt. That fear, of what his life would be like if he didn't have his millions in the bank was real.

"—think, Riley?"

He startled at Tom's use of his name; he'd clearly gone way too far into his own head there.

"Sorry? Can you say that again?"

"We're out on the boat with the survey teams today, you want me to hold off until we know what Santone are down here for?"

"No, carry on as normal, Kathy has feelers out, and I think I might suggest dinner with Josiah, get his intentions out of him when he's drunk too much whiskey."

"Okay, boss."

————

THE BUREAU WAS PISSED. OR AT LEAST MICK STRATTEN FROM

BOEM was pissed. He was Riley's liaison, working with Tom, and they'd gotten to know each other enough that they knew the names of each other's kids. They'd never actually met in person, but he was a straight shooter, as committed as Riley to utilizing the ocean for energy.

"This company is offering incentives for the rights to extract oil."

"Bribes?"

"I didn't use that word, but *incentives* are on the table." Mick cursed.

"What can I do to help?"

"Talk to him, find out what he's doing."

Riley had a sneaking suspicion that Santone was piggy-backing off his and Tom's research. That opened up a whole new can of worms. Who had been sharing the information? He crossed to his door and looked out. From this angle he could see past Kathy's desk and to the main office, where staff did whatever Kathy made them do to make CH work. Someone out there was sharing information and this wasn't the first time it had happened to him.

Sighing, he listened to Mick ranting about Santone, and investments, and what they needed to do to circumvent the crap. Riley heard himself promising to talk to Josiah on an informal basis and sound him out. Great. Just what he wanted to do. When the call ended Riley closed his eyes for a moment. Dinner with Josiah, needed to happen, but Jack was going to be a hard man to convince. He walked out to Kathy's desk and stood in front of it, waiting for her to look up. She'd been in on the conference call to take notes so she'd heard it all.

"Riley?"

"We need to get someone in to track down who is passing on information to—"

"Done, John McMillan at the HART Agency has been highly recommended. I put a call into him."

"Also can you—?"

"Arrange dinner, liaise with Jack and convince him he wants to wear a suit and go to a dinner with a man he dislikes intensely, oh and while I'm at it dig for some more dirt?" She tapped her notebook. "Already on the list."

Oh Jack was really going to hate this, so much.

"Make sure its somewhere that does a good steak," Riley reminded her.

She turned the pad so he could see, next to Jack's name was one word. *Steak*.

CHAPTER 15

*J*ack straightened his tie, tugged his shirt, fiddled with his cuffs, and then held his hands out in front of him and stretched the jacket.

"You look just fine." Riley brushed a hand across his shoulders. "More than fine, hot, sexy, I love you in a suit."

Jack did one more pass over his tie and sighed so loudly the horses in the barn probably heard him. "I hate suits, I hate fancy dinners, and I'm not really fond of Josiah freaking Harrold, or his wife."

Riley slipped between Jack and the mirror, blocking his view.

"I owe you one," he said, with a soft peck of a kiss. Jack would know that was code for some kind of sexual favor if he wanted it, but he would also understand this was Riley's way of apologizing. They sometimes had very little to say on a subject because they knew each other so well.

"For a meal with this man you owe me a hundred." He tempered the grumpiness with a smile. Riley couldn't resist, after all what sane man would not want to kiss Jack Campbell-Hayes dressed up in a dark suit, clean-shaven and with his hair styled just like Riley adored, all kinds of soft. He cradled Jack's face, rubbing his thumbs across his cheekbone, inhaling the scent of the man he loved.

"Thank you," he said.

"What's the code word to escape?" Jack asked, tongue-in-cheek.

"Aliens?"

"How the hell would I fit aliens into a conversation?"

"I don't know, like, Connor says he saw an alien yesterday, or Lexie was abducted by aliens, or you could ask them what they thought of aliens in general."

Jack bit his lip but couldn't hold back a laugh. "Then they'll think we're not right in the head, talking about our kids being abducted by aliens."

They kissed then, both minty fresh from having brushed their teeth, and Riley wanted to kiss that taste away, until it was just him and Jack. They had to separate, the restaurant was in the city, near Love Field, where Josiah had flown into, and it was a good hour from there.

Riley did a mental head count as he left the house. Max was in his room, had vanished there after dinner, clutching a glazed donut and with Toby trailing right behind him. Riley doubted that Max would actually eat the donut and that one sneaky black lab wouldn't get to it first but Carol, super nanny, promised to keep an eye on things. Connor and Lexie were both at the kitchen table doing homework; a worksheet on Canada that Connor was meticulously coloring in, and Lexie was doodling on. The twins were so different; Connor quiet, careful and considered, Lexie a firebrand who couldn't be held back. They were like the two sides of Jack, the quiet part that watched and learned, and the fiery side that had burned his way into Riley's life.

He filed away that thought, alongside other things he'd noticed about the children, like how Max's love for mac 'n cheese seemed to be waning in favor of tomatoes, and how Hayley looked so grown up when she FaceTimed them from college. Jack drove them, singing along with the music on the radio, a mix of music that the kids liked, probably on a station from when they'd last gone out as a family. Lexie was in love with all things Justin Bieber, Connor pretended he hated that sort of thing, but Riley had caught him on more than one occasion singing along.

"You realize you know all the words to that Bieber song," Riley commented as they drew closer to the airfield.

"It's burned into my brain, I think we listened to it ten times in a row on the way to ballet."

Riley glanced sideways at his smiling husband. Jack would listen to Bieber over and over if it meant Lexie was happy. He'd do anything for the children, including being face-painted like a rabbit, playing games with Connor, and braiding Lexie's hair. He knew that Jack found it difficult to connect to Max all the time, but Max was a complicated kid, and the two of them spent most of their alone time with the horses. In fact, Max had stopped calling Jack anything but *Horsy* a few weeks back.

His cell vibrated and he checked it, saw a text from Kathy with the contact details for a John McMillan at the HART agency, and sighed.

"What is it?"

"Someone at CH is passing on the research we're doing, seems as if every time we work a project Santone is there all up in our faces. I need to be really grown up and stop this."

"Adulting is hard," Jack said, supportively, but with humor in his voice. "Maybe we could get Josiah to tell us who is passing it over."

"Yeah, right, like he'd tell us to our faces. That was why we need to get someone in who can track them down and I can shut down that communication."

"You have over a hundred people working for you now, surely…" Jack shrugged.

"Yeah, I don't want to think that any of them would want to fuck CH over."

They made it to the restaurant twenty minutes early and Jack decided he really needed the bar, way more than Riley needed it.

"I don't have to be sober to look pretty as your trophy wife," Jack said as he ordered a whiskey.

"I'm not arguing, but you look pretty all the time." Riley tried to keep his voice down, but the girl organizing the drinks sent them a look that spoke volumes, like how cute that was. He and Jack got that a lot, alongside the infrequent but nasty comments. Sue them all, Jack was his and if he wanted to kiss the man in public then he damn well would. When Josiah Harrold arrived the whole restaurant knew about it, he was just one of those men who demanded everyone *see* him. He laughed loudly, he talked fast and about subjects he held dear, like who he was, what he did and who he'd destroyed to get there. He was old guard and Riley had several run-ins with him on record already.

"Stay calm." Jack gripped his hand. For all his talk of needing a drink he'd nursed the whiskey and only taken a few sips.

"Your table is ready Mr. Campbell-Hayes, and your guests are here." The manager looked pointedly at Josiah and his wife posturing around at the entrance. "We took the liberty of placing you in the blue room where you can be assured of privacy." How the manager kept a straight face as he explained that, Riley didn't know, but he caught the twitch of a smile on Jack's face. Probably more like keeping the Harrolds away from the guests who wanted a quiet meal. This restaurant was a series of small spaces, and he and Jack had eaten in the blue room before, with its own staff, and special menus, then there was this larger area with a bar. Everyone was watching Josiah cross over to them. Sometimes he stopped and shook hands with someone he knew, making sure everyone saw just how connected he was. Finally, he reached Riley and Jack, Dilys trailing him in a cloud of perfume and her face stretched from what appeared to be more plastic surgery, laughing at something Josiah had said. Loudly, like braying. Riley had the uncharitable thought that if her skin was any more stretched it might split, so maybe she shouldn't laugh at all.

Riley held out a hand. "Josiah."

"Hayes," Josiah said. And there it was, the first slap down of the night.

"Campbell-Hayes," Jack said smoothly and shook Josiah's hand firmly. Possibly a little too firmly, but Riley wasn't going to argue. Riley greeted Dilys with two air kisses, which Jack copied, and then the manager led them to the blue room. He noticed that Dilys already had her hand on Jack's arm. She did that a lot, it was her job, to be the wife who flirted and cajoled and generally looked good. Jack may well have described himself as the trophy wife, but there was nothing false about Jack.

Seated, Josiah ordered an obscenely expensive wine, without consulting anyone. "And a steak, the largest you have, bloody," he added to the waiter who nodded without comment.

It seemed like they were actually ordering.

"I'll have a salad, no dressing," Dilys said, and patted Jack's hand, "we have to look after our figures, right Jack?"

Jack smiled. Or rather, he grimaced and forced his lips to curve upward "Steak," he said to the waiter, "rare."

"I'll have the same." Riley reached for Jack's hand under the table. They could do this. Together, holding hands, they could do anything.

They exchanged family news, but didn't get much past the whole JJ is a wonderful son thing that Josiah had going on. All bluster and excitement, he talked about JJ's upcoming wedding, his new dog, losing his license for an unfortunate DUI where he'd clearly been framed. Josiah and Dilys' other kids were conveniently not spoken about. It used to be this way with Riley's dad, or who he thought was his dad. Gerald Hayes had very little time for Riley, or for Eden, mostly focused on Jeff, the oldest. After the fact it became obvious why, given Riley wasn't his son, and Eden was a girl. For both things they were punished with lack of affection or attention.

Jeff was the JJ of the Hayes family, something that Jack had picked up on when he'd first met Josiah.

The steaks arrived, Josiah drank the wine, Jack still had his whiskey, and Dilys sipped noisily at tonic water, poking at her salad as if there were calories hiding in the lettuce that might jump out and hit her. Jack at least enjoyed his dinner.

"Good steak," he said.

Riley mumbled his agreement but every mouthful of his tasted like ash. He hated confrontations, where he'd used to thrive on them when he was younger. But, right now, he wished he was back at the D, with the kids, and Jack, and some box set with a cup of coffee in his hand.

"So," Josiah sat back in his seat, holding the last glass full of wine and looking smug. "What did you want to talk about, Hayes?"

Riley could lie, he could say this was social, but everyone at this table knew it wasn't. He hadn't finished his steak, just placed his cutlery on the plate and pushed it away.

"I had an interesting call on Monday from the Bureau of Ocean Energy Management, wanting to talk about a new project of mine."

Josiah nodded, "Thought they might when there were

two of us looking into the feasibility of that area. What did they say?" He didn't look as if he cared. If anything, he still had a smug expression and Riley wouldn't have put it past him to have sicced the federal government on BOEM to cause the issue. *He knows, I can see it in his eyes.*

"Nothing too bad," Riley lied, "at least nothing we can't handle. The hydropower project is gaining momentum. Our new report submitted today summarized the various potential alternative energy technologies available and screened out unlikely candidates, such as oil extraction in that area."

"Screened out, what do you mean—?"

Riley carried on. "We reported on the general operating principles of each alternative energy technology considered, including reliance on oil, and the current development status of each. Of course, when we wrote the report we didn't expect that Santone would be looking at the same tract of seabed for their oil extraction."

If he hadn't been staring quite so intensely at Josiah's face Riley may have missed the significant tightening of his lips and the narrowing of his eyes.

"Interesting," Josiah said, without pause. "I was led to believe that despite the reports federal agencies are veering away from the recommendations of the Bureau of Ocean Energy Management."

"Not at all, Josiah, I believe that BOEM has been able to smooth over any panic regarding funding and cost against benefit," Riley said, with a nod that underscored his commitment. "I invested some time in explaining our long-term aims and sustainability, and all federal agencies were reassured."

Josiah's lips thinned again and his smile looked more stretched than Dilys'. "There's nothing that says there isn't the option of two alternative uses of the land and water." Josiah placed his wine on the table. He sat forward, his posture stiff, "if you think I am going to sit here and listen to your new age nonsense then you are sadly mistaken, Hayes."

"Not at all," Riley said, and loved that Jack squeezed his hand. "There is room for all kinds of energy extraction, I just think that the extensive research undertaken by CH consulting has proved that hydropower is an effective use of existing tides and land reach, and that stripping the parcels of land there for oil is counterintuitive. Of course, that was only enhanced with the new information we have. Regardless, I'm sure your own research came across the same issues." He said the last innocently, even though he was convinced that somehow Santone Corp had their hands on CH intelligence and reports and had done nothing at all on their own initiative. That was part two on this devious list of his.

Josiah stood from the table, not dramatically but forceful enough to send the chair back a little. "We're leaving, Dilys."

Dilys looked up at her husband and seemed about to say something, probably that she hadn't finished her salad, which vanished instantly. She stood as well, as did Jack and Riley. Never let it be said they lost their Texas good manners in the face of an asshole like Josiah. His idiocy wasn't her fault. Still, they didn't really get to say goodbye in any sense of the word, and were left with an empty room and the check.

"Tell me again how was this a useful way to spend a Thursday evening," Jack deadpanned.

"With any luck Josiah will do two things. One, he'll try and bribe the committee for the work, and they will run him out of town, and two, he'll contact the person who is feeding him information from CH, and give us an idea of who it is."

Jack leaned toward Riley, carding his fingers through Riley's hair. "I love your devious mind." He kissed him briefly and then leaned back in his chair. "I guess we could order dessert now?"

"Or," Riley began carefully, softly into Jack's ear for only him to hear. "We could go home, find some dessert in the fridge and I could lick it off your cock?"

Jack stood so fast that his chair hit the wall yanking Riley up with him. "Home," he growled. "Now."

And Riley wasn't going to argue with that order.

Not at all.

CHAPTER 16

*R*iley drove home, and for that Jack was relieved, not because he'd drunk the whiskey, which he clearly hadn't, but because he couldn't think much past the words dessert, cock, and Riley.

So his smaller brain was in control of everything, including a need for Riley to drive faster.

"Does this heap not go any faster?" he groused, when they were still a few miles away from the D. Jack's cock refused to soften, even when he thought about things like his great aunt Lulu who, he recalled, wore a lot of violet and smelled of cigarettes. Nope, not even that image erased the one he had in his head of Riley on his knees sucking him off.

"You want me to get pulled over for speeding?" Riley chuckled.

The fucker.

"You could do some more," Jack almost whined, and that was not a sexy sound, particularly when Riley laughed. Out loud.

He was so going to pay for that, the bastard.

They made it home to a quiet house, the kids in bed and

Carol in her apartment. Everything had been locked up, there was nothing they needed to do, and Jack went straight to the fridge, pulling out cream and a squeezy bottle of strawberry sauce, courtesy of Connor who lived for the red stuff on every dessert he ate.

Then, when Riley had checked they were all locked in, Jack dragged him into the bedroom and shut the door, locking it so that, hell, no one was getting in here.

"You have to be quiet," Jack said. "Clothes off."

Riley quirked a smile. "I thought I was the one doing this."

Jack placed the sauce and cream on the side table with deliberate care. "Clothes. Off."

Riley did as he was told, but too freaking slowly, removing each item and hanging his suit up, ensuring the jacket sat well, and there were no wrinkles. Meanwhile Jack shoved off his suit and laid it on the back of the chair, and then waited, fisting his cock as he watched his husband strip.

There was a lot of deliberate bending over from Riley and a few coy smiles, and oh yeah, the sin bank was collecting a lot of debt there.

Maybe they should have taken this to the barn. At least in there any noise Riley made would be lost in the dark night, muffled by the insulation that Jack himself had installed. No, there was no way they were leaving this room now, Riley would have to do as he was told. Just the thought of that had Jack coming close to rubbing one out over Riley taking his clothes off. Such was the power of six four of sexy as sin Riley.

Finally, he was naked, and for a few seconds Jack stared at him, then he nodded toward the bed. Riley climbed on and sat in the middle, one hand around the other wrist. Jack had seen that unconscious touch before, and knew what it meant even if Riley didn't. That was what he wanted, to be tied down, to be held and for Jack to do anything he wanted.

Jack could get with that program, and he pulled the soft rope out of the locked drawer that held all kinds of interesting things. They'd used ties before for this kind of play, but after the years they'd been together, the right kind of fastening was enough to make everything easy.

Riley's eyes widened, but he knew better than to say anything. In one smooth move, he lay back on the bed, stretching his arms above him and widening his legs. He would stay like that if Jack wanted him to, his concentration levels were intense when they were making love, but Jack didn't want Riley to have to think tonight. A deft knot, and one of Riley's hands was tied to the bed, another, and his other hand was fixed in place. For a few moments, Jack considered the ankle issue. Tied down, Riley wouldn't be able to move at all or wrap his legs around Jack if they fucked, but he could always untie them. Right?

Two more ties and Riley was still, looking up at Jack, his lips parted and tension seeping out of him.

"God, you're beautiful," Jack whispered, straddling Riley and placing a hand on either side of Riley's head. "You thinking about not moving huh?"

"Yeah," Riley murmured back.

"No sound. Okay?"

Riley nodded and then wriggled, his hard cock brushing against Jack's. He stilled immediately, but not quick enough that Jack didn't add that minor transgression as an extra five minutes of edging.

Jack moved back a little, resting back on Riley's thighs, and then focused on Riley's nipples; at first tracing them, rolling them, and then becoming more insistent, tugging until they were hard, before reaching for the cream, trickling a small path around one nipple. He caught it with his tongue as it slid down Riley's side, and he sucked hard on the small nub, enjoying the taste of the cream and the skin, and hearing the muffled groan as Riley arched into the touch before catching himself.

"Stop thinking about moving." Jack stopped sucking, pressing his hands onto Riley's chest. "Or do I need to tie you across here?

Riley sank into the bed, out of it as Jack concentrated on his nipples, every so often tipping some cream, trickling it down his chest into his navel. Riley was fit, even with some softness from being behind a desk his muscles were defined, just not a six-pack. Still, the cream collected, and licking it away then sucking and nipping at the skin was getting Riley worked up. He was trying his hardest not to move, and Jack wanted him to give in, to stop thinking, that was when he knew Riley was compliant without a head full of worries.

He nipped at the hip bones, his chin bumping Riley's cock on each pass. Each time Riley moaned soft and low and then, blessedly, he began to move. He pressed up against any part of Jack he could get to, attempting to find friction, and getting nothing. Jack dripped cold cream on his cock, watching it slip down and under, onto Riley's balls, following the track of it with his tongue before he closed his mouth over the tip and tugged. Riley moaned again, and Jack recognized the sound. Riley was close just from this.

And Jack did what he wanted there, he backed off and saw the change in Riley's expression from lust to frustration. But he didn't say one single word. Jack waited a moment and then began again, this time with the sauce and the cream, licking and sucking and tasting every inch of Riley, he used his mouth and his hands and brought Riley to the edge a few more times, until there was no hesitation in Riley's movements; he was past thinking.

He slicked his fingers, crooked them inside Riley just to the right point, and swallowed Riley's cock until it hit the back of his throat. He held still for a moment and then set a rhythm, sucking hard as he pressed against Riley.

Riley didn't know where to push, up into Jack's mouth or down, and he was moaning, but it was from somewhere deep inside him, he had no control of anything.

When he came his moan was louder, but nothing that anyone outside of the room would hear. Jack swallowed it all, and then got himself off as Riley twisted on the bed.

He wiped as much away as he could of the sticky sauce residue, untied Riley, and rubbed his wrists, checking if they were marked. Nothing. Riley was like soft toffee, a melted puddle in the bed, boneless and half asleep. Jack padded over to the door and unlocked it; they never locked their door when they were in bed in case the kids needed them. Then he eased boxers onto Riley and himself, just in case, pulled a blanket up over them and slept.

Riley had needed that, hell, Jack had needed that.

And he had to remember to replace the strawberry sauce, which he promptly forgot in sleep.

Which wasn't good when at dinner the next day, with a bowl of ice cream on the table, Connor opened the fridge door and then shut it with a moody push.

"Hey, where's my strawberry sauce!"

CHAPTER 17

*J*ohn McMillan was a big man, taller than Riley, and when Riley had first met him, he'd had an immediate reaction of disbelief that John could be capable of deception as a PI because he stood out too damn much. Six-foot-six and built like a brick shithouse, he filled the sofa in Riley's office, and there wasn't much room left for anyone else. Tattoos wrapped his arm, and he had this menacing way of just sitting. But when he put on a suit and tie and hid the tattoos, he somehow morphed into this gentle giant that people opened up to.

At the moment he was impassive, the information folder laying on the table between him and Riley.

"What do you want to do with it?" he asked.

"What are the options?"

John stared at him steadily; his dark eyes had an absolute laser focus. "Cops, private talk, or vigilante justice."

Riley stared at him and knew his mouth was open. Vigilante justice?

Then John grinned, and the menacing man became something very different. "I was joking about the vigilante thing."

"Oh," Riley began, not wanting to appear stupid in front of this guy who intimidated the hell out of him. "No, I knew that."

"So yeah, we call the cops, or you can bring him in and talk to him."

"It's a 'him'?"

John nudged the papers closer to him. "It's all in there."

Riley didn't want to pick it up; didn't want to know who was doing this to him, to CH. Was it one of the people who'd been here a while? Or one of the IT guys, or an intern working their way through college. Riley felt sick. He'd felt sick since he realized someone here was betraying CH, and him, because he was CH to the core, it was his baby.

"You want me to read it out?" John asked, and shuffled forward a bit, causing the sofa to creak.

"No." Riley picked up the file, and held it steady and unopened. "I'll do it," he said, and then finally flicked to page one. There was a lot of information in here, profiles of his staff that he refused to read, but the main purpose of this, the person who was sharing information with Santone was in full detail on page one.

"Edward Grey, Intern," John said, but Riley could read it all for himself.

And the most damning part of it all. Edward Grey was sleeping with JJ Harrold, Josiah's son.

"You want me to leave?" John asked, but he didn't move. Clearly, he could stay there and play the part of the intimidating muscle, and right now that was what Riley needed.

"No, I'll get...deal..." Riley stood and, shoulders back, he left the office, winding his way through the desks and arriving at Edward's desk, but there was no sign of him.

"He called in sick, sir," Precious Lenwin, Edward's fellow intern piped up, "Think he might have the flu that's going around. Can I help you with something?"

"No, thank you." Riley backed away and stepped right into John. They exchanged glances and Riley was suddenly determined to get this done. He stalked back across the office and to Kathy's desk. "I'm out," he said, and with John behind him, he left the building. "I guess you have an address," he said, aware he was being an ass, but also understanding his temper was justified. Edward was a good kid, in his final year in business school at UT, recommended by a friend. He'd gone through the normal vetting, and Riley trusted him as he trusted every employee. He didn't argue when John guided him to a large black SUV and gestured for Riley to get in.

Within thirty minutes they were across the city, and outside a block that looked way beyond an intern's means.

"Wait, isn't this JJ's place?" Riley asked as he stared up at the glass and stone building.

John nodded, followed just behind Riley as he walked inside and headed straight for security in the lobby.

"JJ Harrold," Riley said, very simple and to the point. "No, he's not expecting me, and yes, he will see me. My name is Riley Campbell-Hayes."

The man on duty glanced from Riley to John, who stood there all big and scary. He was no doubt contemplating calling the cops, and Riley sighed.

"JJ will see me," he said again.

The man picked up the handset and rang a number. "Sir, there is a Riley Campbell-Hayes for you… Yes…absolutely I can do that… Yes, sir." He replaced the handset and moved to the elevator, using a key card to open it, and gesturing them in. "Six," he said, and then backed away. The elevator ride was smooth and quick, and when the door opened at six, which Riley assumed was the entire floor, the lobby was marble tile and quiet.

Then a door opened, and JJ walked out, stopping at the door and waiting.

"Before you say anything," he began and held up a hand. "Listen to me."

Riley wasn't in the mood to listen. "Is Edward here?"

A second man appeared behind JJ, shorter, and he looked as if he'd been crying, and Riley saw red. Had JJ used his position of authority to use Edward, just as he'd tried to do with Tom?

Where the punch came from, Riley didn't know for sure, his anger at the fact he'd been betrayed, the fact that it was JJ, the fact that Josiah-fucking-Harrold was getting right up in CH's business, and Riley was done.

JJ sprawled back, catching himself on the door jamb, so as not to end up on the floor.

"Riley, stop!" JJ shouted and held out a hand. Riley felt every ounce of anger flood to his clenched fist, but Edward moved to stand between Riley and JJ and, shoulders back, he defied the man who signed his paycheck.

"Leave him alone!" he yelled. He was still crying, but this was in anger and a hint of desperation.

Riley backed away, surprised, shocked, seeing JJ's hand on Edward's shoulder, and the naked fear and love on his face. He'd seen that before, in the looks Jack gave him, and abruptly all the anger dissipated. He felt a hand on his own shoulder.

"I think you have this now." John headed back for the elevator.

"Come in," JJ said, and he and Edward went inside leaving the door open.

Riley followed them, casting a quick look at his surroundings, at the view of the city, the high ceilings, the obscenely expensive feel of the whole place, and then the boxes. Three of them. Open, with items sticking out; clothes, and books and at the top of the nearest one was a photo frame and in there a picture of Edward and JJ.

"What the fuck is going on. Edward, if he's hurting you, we can work this out—"

"He's not hurting me." Edward moved into JJ's arms.

Riley couldn't understand this. He knew JJ, and the bastard was a chip off the old block, hell, he'd tried it with Tom, and Tom had punched him and then lost his job. JJ was Santone Oil, the heir, the one who would take their blustering, bloated company into the future. He'd never liked him, even if they'd been drinking buddies way back, it was proximity, never friendship, and when Riley met Jack he wasn't *that* man anymore that was anything like JJ.

"I wouldn't hurt him; I love him. You'd better sit down, Riley."

Riley took the nearest seat, and Edward and JJ sat opposite, holding hands. Riley wasn't going to believe a word of this and looked at Edward, willing him to meet his eyes so he could see exactly what was going on. Was Edward being blackmailed?

"I don't know where to start," JJ said.

Riley didn't even offer the usual response to that, the beginning, because talking right now, when he was still angry and confused, wasn't a good idea. Part of him, the needy part, wished Jack was here, because he'd be a steadying influence. Riley noticed the redness of JJ's face, and the fact that it would bruise up around his eye.

"So the Hayes and the Harrolds, hell, you know as well as I do that our dads hated each other, for reasons I never understood, or cared to understand. Rivalry, money, who had the biggest house, the prettiest wife, the best children, it was like some fucking kids' playground with the two of them." He looked to Edward for something, reassurance that he was doing things right, probably. Edward shoulder-bumped him, offering a smile and finally meeting Riley's gaze.

"And?" Riley prompted.

"I was born into that, same as you were, but I never found my Jack, do you get that? So the poison festered, and it made me a man who...hell, I don't even know what it made me, a waste of space. I expected I could have everything, and I took what I wanted, and I drank. A lot. Same as you, only you found Jack."

"You keep saying that," Riley began.

JJ held up a hand. "Please, let me get this out," he said. "But then, we were failing, missing out on bids, losing to your ethical solutions, and dad wanted blood. He said we needed intel, that I should get you in bed, shit he was insane, as if that would ever happen. You have Jack."

He paused, and gripped Edward's hand. "Our plan, his plan, get inside, approach Tom maybe, but there was no way... so I focused in on an intern, Edward, used him, hurt him." He looked at Riley, and his eyes were bright with emotion. "But, I fell in love, and Edward made me see what I could be...and I'm leaving Santone; I won't work there anymore."

"We'll start over somewhere else," Edward said, with confidence.

Riley processed what he could, and sat back in his seat. "Explain everything, from the beginning, slowly."

RILEY SKIPPED GOING BACK TO THE OFFICE, WANTED TO GO home, needed to see Jack, thankful he owned the company and could disappear for the last few hours of the day. He had an idea of where Jack would be, over at the school, knowing that Thursday at four in the afternoon was Max's riding lesson and that they had a half an hour before that to talk.

"Is Jack around?" he asked Liam, who didn't look away from some intricate work on a saddle, and waved in the general direction of the office. Riley hurried over, knocked on the closed door and went in before Jack even said a word. Jack glanced up surprised, but the polite smile gave way to a broad grin, and he was up on his feet in an instant and pulling Riley in for a hug.

"What are you doing here?" he asked with a smile, "Not that it isn't good to see you in the middle of the day."

"We found out who was passing information to Santone."

Jack's expression changed to one of sympathy, and he squeezed Riley quickly. "Who?"

"An intern, Edward, remember you met him at the Fourth of July picnic?"

"Short, skinny, blond, I remember him. What the hell, Riley?"

"He's sleeping with JJ, and—"

"I'll kill him," Jack muttered, "Fucking JJ and his shit."

"No, listen. He's changed, and he's in love with Edward, and they're running off to get married, and his dad will kill him when he finds out, and I said I'd cover for him if I needed to, if it helped, and Jack?"

Jack looked at him as if he'd gone mad. "What?" he finally asked.

"You know how he convinced me he was in love with Edward?"

"How?" The words dripped with suspicion.

"He told me he'd met his Jack."

"Oh." Jack cradled Riley's face. "Oh," he repeated again.

"He's been passing the wrong information to Josiah for a while now, and that's why what Josiah is doing lately is always slightly off. We should be thanking him."

Jack snorted a laugh. "Thank the man who slept with one of your interns to gather intel on how to win bids that you have spent months planning? Yeah right."

Riley kissed him then, kissing away the laughter, and

pressing him back against the desk. They wouldn't be thanking him, of course, but there was one thing that had made Riley stop and think.

Finding his Jack had made him a better man, and JJ had found *his* Jack in Edward.

And for that, Riley seemed to be able to forgive JJ and Edward both.

Because finding love in weird situations? Well, Riley understood that, completely.

CHAPTER 18

*H*ayley came home for Jack's forty-fifth birthday, arriving a couple of days before and planning to stay a week. She was nearly done with her third year at college now, and she'd come home loaded down with books and notepads and holed herself up in her room for the entire first day of her visit. She'd worked at CH in the summer the previous year, and was likely to join the company again in a couple of weeks, after her exams which loomed over her. Her workload was incredible, and Jack couldn't help her with any of it. Riley went up several times with drinks and snacks and then didn't come down for an hour at a time. He could help her with geophysics, which was a module that both Riley and Hayley found fascinating.

If she seemed quiet and pale, Jack didn't like to comment on it, but he did worry that maybe she was doing too much. Also, he noticed she'd ignored five calls from Logan, turning her phone over.

What the hell was going on there?

The next morning she was having breakfast, still tired and pale, and on the verge of a hypo. He didn't say anything as she ate cereal and counted the carbs, making a note on her phone and tutting.

"Everything okay?" he asked when she tutted again and slammed her phone down onto the table. She didn't do that; her phone was her life, and possibly smashing it wasn't something she would do.

She shot him a look that spoke volumes. "I hate having this stupid disease," she snapped, "I wake up, my sugars are low, and I feel as if I haven't slept, I'm muddled and irritable, I'm running out of time for the exams, and I don't understand what I'm reading when I'm on the verge of a freaking hypo, and..." the steam in her escaped in a frustrated sigh and then she buried her face in her hands. A hypo, short for hypoglycemia, was one of the worst parts of having diabetes.

Jack considered where Riley was, because Riley knew about college and exams and all that side of Hayley. But God, diabetes or not, she was so much like Riley in the way she let stress build and build until there was nowhere for it to go. With Riley he went quiet and hid away, and right on cue Hayley stood, rinsed her bowl and put it in the dishwasher.

"I'm going to study," she announced.

Nope, this wasn't a Riley situation; this was something that Jack was going to handle.

"No, you're not," Jack said, and moved so he was blocking the door out of the kitchen.

"Pappa, I need to study."

"Not this morning."

She pushed at him; she still had that slightly uncoordinated look that came with her sugars still climbing to whatever was normal for her. Her push was nothing.

"Let's go riding," he said. "I'll pack some snacks, and we'll visit Legacy, go up on the bluff, Red's been missing you."

At the use of her horse's name, she faltered a little and then that steely Riley-Hayes look sparked in her eyes.

"No, Pappa, I came back for your birthday, and I already lost four days just for that, you have to let me study."

Jack wasn't going to let himself be hurt by her words. They meant nothing, but he was scared for the bags under her eyes and her pale skin. Did she ever see the outside of a study room? Wasn't geology all about going out and observing rocks, surely she should be out in the sun.

"Turn around, and I'll meet you at the barn.

Frustration had her balling her fists, and she tried to evade him, but her sluggish reflexes were no match for a determined father.

"Out. Barn. Saddle up Red."

"No. You can't make me; I'm twenty-one, not ten anymore."

"As long as you're under my roof you'll do what I say." Even as Jack said the words, he cringed at the sound of his momma's voice telling him that when he tried to get away with shit when he was at home.

"I'll talk to Dad," Hayley warned.

Jack laughed. He couldn't help it. Hayley and her siblings had ever had any success in playing their parents off against each other, and it wouldn't start now. Of course, laughing was the very first thing on the list of what not to do in the parent's handbook, and he instantly regretted it, when her eyes filled with tears.

Tears he couldn't handle.

"Just let me study today," she wheedled, and one perfect tear slid down her face. Master manipulation; she'd done it at ten, and she was an expert now.

But Jack was determined.

"Barn, Hayley, Red."

She stared up at him. He didn't back down. She turned, muttering under her breath, and left the house. He saw her pass the window and was thankful that at least she was heading for the barn. Robbie was out there, and he'd help her if she needed it, not that she did, but he'd be there to listen just how awful her Pappa was. He needed to get used to that kind of thing with Louise and Jeremy getting older.

When he went to the barn, he saddled Kalli, a mare out of Solo's line, and mounted, waiting just outside the stable for Hayley. She emerged on her horse, and wouldn't look him in the eyes, but did at least follow him away from the ranch and to the bluff. Jack halted and dismounted, scruffing Kalli's mane and waiting for something to happen.

Because just like with Riley, something always did.

She didn't get off Red, she sat there, a stubborn set to her chin, staring out over the ranch, but subtly it changed. She was thinking, processing, going over everything, and then she dismounted and came to stand in front of Red, right next to Jack.

He pulled her into his side, and waited for her to talk, to get everything off her chest about college and whatever else it was that was stressing her out.

But she shocked him, she burst into tears, and he had to hold her up and, fuck, what the hell was happening? He held her close, her height put her head at the base of his chin, and he didn't let go of her, not until the sobs became little more than harsh breathing and finally, peace.

"You don't have to talk," Jack began softly, "but you know your dad and I, we're always here for you."

She looked up at him, her hazel eyes bloodshot and swimming with tears.

"I had a scare," she said, and gripped his shirt, "I thought I was pregnant, I mean, I was…" she dipped her head.

"Oh Hayley, baby."

"Please don't be disappointed."

"Hayley?" Jack pressed a finger to her chin to tilt her face, so she looked at him. "Nothing you might do could ever disappoint me." He stepped away and pulled the blanket from his horse and laid it on the ground under the nearest Texas Ash tree, along with the drinks and snacks. "Sit down, sweetheart."

She did, and watched him as he sat cross-legged facing her.

"I missed a period, and used a pregnancy test, and then I had an early pregnancy loss, there was a lot of bleeding, and I was scared."

"I'm so sorry, why didn't you call?"

"Because I'm at college and these things don't happen, not to me."

"What did Logan say?" He assumed it was Logan, as last time they'd both visited he'd caught his daughter and Logan in a heated kiss and had backpedaled so fast out of the room he'd tripped over Toby and fallen onto the wall. Awkward.

She shook her head, and he didn't understand what she was trying to say. Had Logan been with her? He wouldn't have let her go through this alone.

"Hayley?"

"Ididn'ttellhim," she mumbled. Then she closed her eyes. "I didn't tell him, okay. I avoided his calls, and now I've fucked everything up and I can't talk to him at all, and he's coming here tomorrow and I've managed to put him off, but it's your birthday."

Oh shit. She's done a Riley, and hidden everything away.

Jack hoped to hell that Logan channeled some of his Uncle Jack, because Hayley needed to be pulled out of her own head sometimes, just like Riley.

"Don't tell dad, please, Pappa."

Jack shook his head. "We don't keep secrets," he said. "You know I will tell him, unless you tell him first, baby."

"I can't." Fresh tears accompanied those words. "He'll be so disappointed, and—"

"Stop projecting your own fears onto other people, Hayley." He must have sounded super strict because she clamped her mouth shut and there was a hint of mutiny in her expression. He sighed again. "Your dad will hug you, and tell you he'll do anything to make things better, okay? And as to Logan, he deserves to know what happened, and why you're avoiding him. It takes two to make a baby you know."

"I can't," she said, and knotted her hands together in her lap.

He reached over and unknotted them, holding her hands in his and squeezing.

"Let's go back and find your dad, hmm? And then, get Logan over, and talk."

"He'll be so angry I didn't tell him. I'm not sure I can argue or defend myself right now." She looked so confused, and Jack felt as if he wanted to reach inside her and unknot all her fears as easily as he had her hands. But he couldn't do that, not any more than he could with Riley. He could just be there to help.

She pulled out her cell, and wrote a text. "I've asked Logan to come over, if he still wants to."

"He'll want to."

"I love you, Pappa," Hayley said. "Dad and me? We're so lucky to have you."

Jack smiled, and then considered a way of getting her to smile. "I hope that means I'll get a kick-ass present for my birthday."

She glanced sideways and smirked. "I knew I'd forgotten something."

They rode back to the D, via Legacy, stopping for a coffee and by the time they were back home she appeared better, color in her cheeks and a smile on her face. Of course, the smile slipped a little when she saw Riley waiting for them.

"Hey guys, you have fun?" He followed them into the barn.

Hayley dismounted. "Dad, can I talk to you?"

Riley hugged her and allowed himself to be tugged outside, but Jack could see them, over by the fence. He didn't have to watch to know that Riley listened, though, and then pulled Hayley close, but he did watch.

Seeing Riley and Hayley like that made his heart feel light.

Now there was just Logan, whose car pulled to a stop next to Riley's. He stood by the car, probably thinking the worst. If she'd been ignoring his calls, and otherwise avoiding him then he might well have thought she was going to end things. He looked whipped, broken-hearted, and Jack knew at that moment that this was a man deeply in love.

Hayley hugged Riley one last time and they separated, Riley walking over to Jack, Hayley to Logan. He caught Hayley kissing Logan, and then stepping back, talking, but he was distracted when Riley stood next to him. He was sad, blown away, and Jack gripped his shoulder.

"Shit," Riley murmured.

"You okay?" he asked. "Hayley will be fine; she's young, she's learning."

EVERYONE WAS ASLEEP, INCLUDING LOGAN, WHO'D DECIDED HE was staying over on the sofa in the living room—even Riley, who had fallen asleep as soon as his head had hit the pillow. Well, after mutual and very quiet pre-birthday blowjobs of course.

Jack was wide awake, his head buzzing with thoughts. Mainly he wondered if they should have broken the no boys in your room rule, given Hayley's age and the fact that she and Logan were inseparable, but his gut told him that would have been wrong.

So he slept in his comfy bed, and dreamed of birthdays, and horses, and babies who were just like Hayley.

OF COURSE, WHEN HE WOKE UP THE NEXT MORNING, HEADING for the kitchen and coffee he looked into the living room, and Logan was there all right. He was squeezed on the huge sofa. But next to him, clinging tight to Logan in her pajamas, her face smushed into Logan's shoulder was Hayley.

Now that?

That was love.

JACK'S FORTY-FIFTH BIRTHDAY WAS LOUD, AND FUN, AND FULL of gifts; photos, books, a new saddle that Riley had ordered from a custom leather worker they'd found on a trip to San Antonio, and from the kids, he received a new wallet, comedy socks, and a framed photo of all four of them, even Max, which he hung on the wall of his and Riley's bedroom, and of course so many hugs and so much love it was hard to keep score.

Definitely his kind of birthday.

CHAPTER 19

*T*he last year, since his birthday, and that fateful weekend where Hayley had told them about the miscarriage, there had been a new connection with Logan that Jack hadn't appreciated before. He spent a lot of time there on the weekends, talking about life, and the reasons why things happened, and tending to the horses, and maturing before Jack's eyes. He'd spoken a lot about the time in which he and Hayley might have a baby for real.

That was why it didn't surprise him when Logan turned up at the barn early one Saturday morning.

"Uncle Jack, do you have a minute?"

Jack backed his way out of the stall at Logan's voice. The wood was rotted at the back and one good kick from Solo would leave a hole. On his hands and knees, he was applying a temporary mend and adding the full repair to his list of *very important things to do*. He suspected an armadillo had eaten its way in, and he resolved to do something about that.

"Hold this will you?" he asked Logan, who crouched down next to him and held the board in place while Jack screwed and nailed it so that even the most enterprising armadillo would be hard pressed to break in this way. Armadillo 0, Jack 1.

"You should replace the entire back wall."

"Tell me something I don't know," Jack said irritably, he couldn't help it, his to-do list was growing daily, what with Connor and his math wall, Lexie and her ballet medal cabinet, and now Max wanting shelves for his Thomas collection. Today had been designated a family day, but sue him, he'd taken his morning coffee to the new barn, just to check on the horses, nothing too bad, and had found the hole. Or at least Solo, all restless and jumpy in the stall, had found it for him,

"Are you coming into the house now?" Logan asked and sat back on his haunches, staring down at the fixed hole and very definitely not meeting Jack's gaze.

Jack's eyes narrowed on his nephew. He seemed tense. He'd been working with his dad now for two years, still back and forth to UT in Austin, but he was in his last year. It seemed like yesterday that Logan had been fighting for the right to leave New York and come home with his dad, and now Campbell and Campbell was getting closer, and Hayley was in her last year in Denver, and Jack was three years older.

He'd found more gray this morning, a whole mess of the fuckers at his temple, but standing and looking at them wouldn't make them go away.

Anyway, Riley had reassured him there were no signs of gray in his groin, after doing a thorough search and finishing off with one hell of a blowjob.

"Uncle Jack?" Logan said, and Jack took his mind very deliberately away from thoughts of blowjobs and gray hair and back to crouching in a barn with Logan.

"Yep?"

"You coming in for breakfast now?"

"In a bit, why? Is your dad with you?"

Jack peered around Logan, expecting to see Josh standing there; he kind of needed to see his big brother who had way more gray than he did. Teasing him about his hair would make Jack feel way better.

"No, it's just me."

"Okay, are you sure you want to be here around breakfast 'cause you know it's Riley cooking, right?"

Riley and cooking had hit a few snags; he'd come back from a recent trip to a symposium in Italy armed with what seemed like a list of really awesome—his words not Jack's—herbs and spices. It was all Italian-this and Italian-that. No doubt breakfast would come with little red, white and green flags sticking out of the biscuits. Riley was known for burning things still; nothing changed there.

"He sent me over here when I asked if you were here, told me to tell you the smoke alarm needs a new battery."

Jack couldn't help smiling. Riley plus breakfast always resulted in burned something. Burned bacon Jack could handle, all that crunchy goodness, he didn't care how he got his daily fix of bacon. Still, burned toast was so not his thing. Never mind; the whole thing was made with love and that was all that mattered.

He stood and rubbed his hands on his jeans, knowing he'd spent way too much time on the floor even to consider sneaking in without washing up with more than a conciliatory hand wash. Logan scrambled to stand as well, and Jack realized, not for the first time, that somehow the damn kid was taller than him now. Seemed as though he was cursed to be looking up at the men in his life. Not that Logan was a kid, he'd just passed his twenty-sixth birthday, and was now clerking for his dad. Josh was so puffed up with pride that Jack found every chance he got to tease his brother.

According to Josh, Logan was the most amazing son in the history of all sons. Jack agreed for the most part; Logan was one of the good guys, worked hard, knew this family, and really the only cloud on the horizon was the whole dating-Hayley thing. Yes, he'd come to terms with Logan/Hayley, more so than maybe Riley had, but still, it was there whenever they talked about Logan. That hesitation that Hayley could meet someone else and that life wasn't all about Logan.

After all, right now, there were princes out there waiting to get married. Right? And a dad wanted the best for his daughter in love.

"Is everything okay?" Jack asked as he stretched out the aches from last night's particularly athletic session in the shower with a very flexible Riley. Well, shower, then bed, then floor, and table, and that reminded him, he said he'd help Riley clear up all the papers. Of course, he'd been fucking him hard at the time and he'd have said anything to get Riley's head back into sex and away from the oil field maps that tumbled to the floor in chaos.

Last time he'd tried to help Riley sort out paperwork he'd been banned from the office for a month, only allowed in with coffee or cookies in hand. They'd sure got through a lot of cookies in those weeks for Jack to get his near hourly fix of his husband.

"I wanted to talk to you about something really serious, Uncle Jack."

Uh oh, no conversation that started with that kind of introduction was going to be a good one. Jack braced himself for Logan explaining how he wasn't working with Josh anymore and that he was done with law, or some sweeping statement about how he wanted to climb mountains, or paddle boat the Amazon. Because that was what Logan's friends were doing, the ones who sent postcards from exotic locations where they were spending their inheritances. Hayley would be brokenhearted if that happened. It didn't matter that Logan was steady, strong, certain and positive of what he wanted, Jack was skeptical he was different from the rest of his cohorts that Riley told stories about. Riley got most of it from Logan's Facebook, but Jack wasn't one for social media, and Facebook horrified him.

"Okay?"

Logan looked behind, as if he was checking to see if anyone could hear, but when Riley sauntered into the barn, it seemed he'd been waiting for that moment.

"I burned the bacon." Riley stood next to Jack, bumping shoulders. "Left it in the warmer for you."

"Mmmm, bacon," Jack murmured, and they shared a smile.

Logan cleared his throat and shuffled, then did this very obvious thing where he pushed back his shoulders and settled his breathing. He appeared older standing there, more like a young Josh, all kinds of serious and focused.

"Uncle Jack, Riley, I have something very important I want to ask you."

Jack wondered if Riley felt as weird as he did, standing here at 8 a.m., before breakfast, on a Saturday, with the coolness of a Texas morning all peaceful and quiet around them.

Well, apart from a shuffling sound somewhere in the stalls which Jack bet was that freaking armadillo rooting around for food.

"Okay," Riley said, and Jack didn't have to know Riley well to hear the slight hesitation in his voice, the hitch of the word that made Jack want to grab Riley's hand. Was something wrong? Was Logan ill? Was it Josh? Or Anna, or the kids?

"I wanted to do this properly, even though Hayley says I'm being stupid, and I—" Logan stopped, and his shoulders dipped before he caught himself and stood. "I'm just going to say it, okay, then I'm going to leave, and give you time, okay, and then I'll wait, in the kitchen, or I'll drive off and you can call me, or dad. Hayley said I'm old-fashioned, but it's the way I was brought up, and you know that Uncle Jack, because it's your fault as well that I'm like this."

"Logan?" Jack interjected, watching as his now confident nephew stumbled over a mass of words that meant nothing. "Calm down."

Logan took a deep breath and slowly let it out. "Okay," he began, settling his words. "I wanted to ask you for Hayley's hand in marriage."

Jack hadn't been expecting that. Neither had Riley, by the way he stiffened next to him.

"You want to…?" Riley said.

"Marry Hayley." Logan reached into his pocket and pulled out a small box, opened it to reveal a simple band with a diamond. "I have the ring, and we've talked about it, and I think she'd say yes, but it's important to me that you approve, and that you want this and—"

"Lo, stop." Jack held up his hand. Logan subsided and took a step back and away from them. His expression had gone from confident and focused to insecure and he moved back again.

"You need time," he said, and turned to leave.

Jack didn't think that Logan leaving was a good idea; they needed to talk; a man couldn't come in here and drop news like this on them and then walk away. He and Riley had questions to ask, things they needed to know about Logan, his prospects, his promise he would love Hayley and look after her, and make her laugh, and dry her tears, and be there just as Jack and Riley had always tried to be.

"Okay, so this is you respecting us and our opinions, Riley, you agree?"

Riley made a small noise of agreement, and his fingers touched Jack's, and then curled and twisted there to grip hard Jack's hand. How they handled this was vital; it would be the basis for knowing Logan as something other than nephew and boyfriend, but as a man who could cherish their daughter.

Shit, now I'm using words like cherish.

Logan continued with a nod. "I'm a few years away from partner with Dad, with the office I mean, not Dad, I never meant to mention Dad, I meant..." Logan stopped and closed his eyes briefly. "I've saved money, and Hayley's about to graduate and says she'll be working with you. I have great career prospects in a firm that will be rooted in family, and I see as thriving and growing annually. Financially, I have a small trust fund that I'll be inheriting at thirty from Grandma Campbell, and I will look after Hayley and support her." He looked at Riley. "I am not marrying her for money; I can make my own way in the world."

"Logan, stop," this time it was Riley who held up his free hand. "Of course this isn't about money, but, you tell us all this, but you're not telling us the most important thing. How do you feel?"

"Freaking nervous," Logan quipped and then paled, "I mean confident, I mean... I don't know what you mean."

"How do you *feel* about Hayley?"

Jack realized that Riley was picking up on the fact everything Logan had said was all technical detail, all about money and purpose and career. Riley and Jack needed more than this and Logan had one chance to get this right. Not that Hayley would listen to either of her dads if they got all up in themselves and got lost in the fact that to them Hayley was still that little girl that had arrived all those years ago. If she loved Logan, which it was clear she did, then she would marry him whatever. Like Father like daughter.

"Hayley?" Logan said, and then he smiled, his posture relaxed and his smile widened. "I love her more than I could ever explain to her or you. I think about her from the minute I wake up to the moment I fall asleep and then sometimes I dream about her. I promise you I will spend every day making her as happy as I can." He pressed a hand to his chest, right over his heart, and there was passion written in every line of his expression. "It sometimes hurts, the thought of not being with her. I can't imagine a life without her." The words were spoken with such love that it was just like Jack talking about Riley.

"Last week she was making this sandwich," Logan held his hands in front of him as if he was making one himself, "I wanted just to go over and hold her and never let go. Over a damn sandwich. She looked up at me and smiled and my heart, it hurt with what I felt for her. I didn't know I could ever feel like this about another person."

Riley squeezed Jack's hand. If they'd had the time they would have made a decision together, that was how they rolled, but this was here and now, and Logan deserved for them to be honest.

"You first," Jack murmured because, for all the adoption and the fact Hayley was his as much as she was Riley's, it was Riley who hadn't quite got his head around Logan/Hayley as much as he wanted to.

Now it was Riley's turn to clear his throat. He loosened his fingers from Jack's and nodded. Just once, subtle and only caught in Jack's peripheral vision.

"If you ask Hayley, and she says yes, then I couldn't be

happier to have you as a son-in-law," Riley said, all serious, extending his hand to shake Logan's.

Logan gripped Riley's hand, and they shook, and then Riley tugged him close, and the handshake turned into a hug, but not a bro-hug with backslapping. No, this was a desperate hold from Riley, a need to let Logan know through touch alone just how much this moment meant to him. His eyes were closed, and he held Logan so tightly that Jack imagined that he'd have to get in there to pry them apart when Riley released his hold. His beautiful eyes were bright with emotion, but then Logan's were as well, and Jack? He had a lump in his throat the size of Texas.

"Uncle Jack?" Logan asked.

Now it was Jack's turn to pull Logan into a hug, just as desperate and as full of meaning as Riley's.

"Welcome to the family," Jack murmured, and couldn't resist adding. "Again."

When they parted Logan stumbled back, pocketing the ring, "I have to go," he said, and left. Just like that. Gone.

For a few moments they stood in silence.

"You think he's going to ask her now?" Riley asked, and grasped Jack's hand again.

Jack sighed. "On a Saturday morning, without candles, romance, good food and the ring in a champagne glass? I hope not."

Riley huffed a laugh. "We never had all that," he said. "We just had a contract, and the intent to defraud."

Jack caught something in his husband's voice hidden under the humor, a regret maybe? "Yeah, but what we did have is a story to tell the grandchildren one day."

Riley turned to face him then. "I'm handling the proposal right now; don't go adding in grandchildren already."

"Logan's one of the good ones." Jack cradled Riley's face, and Riley pressed against his hand.

"You remember the day she told us she was going to marry Logan? What was she? Ten or something?"

"Yeah, so convinced that Logan was the man she would be with forever."

"You think she knew right from then, that she would love him?"

"I don't know," Jack answered honestly, because Riley was angling for something, some kind of answer that would clear the worries from his expression.

"We never did that either. When we met you were just this man who would help me get what I thought was mine."

"Riley, you need to let go of this, first the proposal, now the fact we didn't fall in love at first sight? What matters is that we soon realized we were meant to be together."

Riley moved closer, and Jack folded him in for a hug, which was always awkward at first with Riley's height. Somehow they had this way of Riley slightly bending his knees, and Jack reaching up, and then Riley burying his face in Jack's neck. They'd done that so many times over the years, they'd found the perfect way to fit together.

"The day I fell in love with you, for real, was the moment Jeff offered you fifteen million to back away," Riley murmured, "It was my mirror moment."

"What?" Jack asked, with affection, leaning back against the stall so he could hold Riley even closer. This big man with his family and memories that shaped him sometimes just needed to be held. And hugged.

"I read about it. That single moment that you look at yourself and realize how desperate you are for things to work a certain way. I would have given everything at that point for you to stay with me, but I didn't do it because I loved you, I needed you."

Riley's voice was muffled against his neck, and Jack nudged him so he lifted his head.

"You so loved me," he teased.

Riley kissed the side of Jack's neck. "I know that now."

"And you'll always love me, because I am just that good."

The small kisses on his skin became little nips, and Jack squirmed away. Trust Riley to do that single thing Jack liked so much to get him harder than iron in what seemed like seconds.

"Good at burning bacon," Jack said with a smirk.

Riley mouthed Jack's earlobe and then whispered. "Good at sucking you, and fucking you."

"And?" Jack feigned boredom, but the instinctive baring of his neck for Riley's kisses belied the presence.

"At loving you. I'll always be the best person at loving you."

There, that is what Jack needed to hear, and he was *so* ready to answer.

"Of course you will, we were always meant to be together, love at first sight or not, we fit."

The kisses turned to more, Jack trying to drag Riley closer, aware that burnt bacon and breakfast or not, their barn was no more than thirty feet away. He wanted to be inside Riley, in his body, his heart; he was impossibly needy whenever it came to Riley, and he could never have enough.

"Dad! Pappa!"

Jack released his grip on Riley and Riley stepped back. They were good at this, the ability to switch from lovers to fathers in a split second. Connor's voice was loud, he wasn't too close yet, but any minute now he would be.

"Lexie spilled milk everywhere, and Toby pulled the bacon off the counter, and he's hiding under the table, and Max is there with him and has a whole carton of orange juice, and you need to come in right now."

"We're coming," Riley said, with a rueful smile, pulling out his shirt to hide the same kind of erection that Jack was sporting. "Later," he said for Jack's ears only.

Then, holding hands, they went into the house.

And all Jack could think when he walked into the chaos, at orange juice on the floor mingling with milk, and one very satisfied dog wagging its freaking tail, was one thing.

Not my bacon.

CHAPTER 20

*R*iley was like a cat on hot bricks. They'd heard nothing from Hayley.

Not a single word.

"I still think we should text her and ask her."

"No, Riley."

"But she knows he asked us, so she'd be expecting our call, right?"

"No."

Riley punched Jack lightly on the arm and Jack feigned pain and grabbed his arm letting out a soft ouch.

Three days had passed since Logan's visit in the barn and the declaration he was going to propose to Hayley, and then nothing. Nada. Zip.

Riley pulled his horse to a stop near the edge of the bluff, and Taylor stopped on a dime. Solo halted as well, and Jack edged her forward, so they were next to each other. The view from here over the ranch was a familiar one, and if they turned to face the other way they would see Legacy Ranch. Beyond their house was the riding school, the fences, newly painted, gleamed white in the dimming light.

"What if she said no?" Riley mused. That was a possibility. She was twenty-two, days away from graduating; maybe she was in love with Logan but wanted to wait.

Jack laughed at that. "This is Hayley, of course, she said yes."

Riley sighed and went back to looking at the view. "So why hasn't she called?"

"Maybe it hasn't happened yet, maybe at her graduation on the weekend? You need to chill and let it happen."

Riley turned to Jack and shook his head. "Says the man who took his cell phone into the shower with him wrapped in plastic, just in case."

Jack smirked. Riley was just as bad, he'd not let his cell out of his sight, and checked his email every five minutes. Tomorrow they were flying up to Denver for Hayley's graduation, Connor and Lexie were coming with them, along with Logan, Donna, Neil, Sandra, and Jim. Riley had chartered a jet for them all, the company jet long since gone after Riley realized how stupid it was for CH to have something like that, for various environmental reasons. But for the graduation he'd decided that they were making this special. Luckily, Jack hadn't argued, and didn't bat an eyelid at the hotel they were all staying in. Everyone else who wanted to see Hayley would have to watch the video Connor had promised to take and then everyone was invited to a huge graduation party back at the ranch in a couple of weeks when she came home.

Home. Here.

Where was she going to live? Would she move into Logan's small place near his work? Would she want a place in Dallas near her work? Would she want to come home? She could come home; her room was still there. It was where she stayed during the holidays, because she was still Riley and Jack's daughter.

But things were different now. She was going to be a

graduate, engaged, and she'd be married and then who knew what life would be like?

Blindly Riley reached for Jack's hand. This was the happiest time of their lives, seeing their daughter start her new life, but fuck, why did it have to be so damn hard?

SEEING HER WALK UP ONTO THE STAGE, RECEIVING HER diploma, shaking hands, listening to speeches and watching her entire year of graduates throw mortarboards into the air was something Riley wouldn't ever forget. He and Jack were bursting with pride, and at that moment in time, when they clapped and cheered for her, he felt as if everything in his world was right.

They met her after the ceremony, hugging her, and Logan was there, hugging her too. Riley had to back away and let him, handing over some of the love she needed to come from him.

The air was hot, the shade given by the huge trees in the grounds of this beautiful campus were welcome, and then it happened.

In front of grandparents, parents, and her sister and brother, Logan went down on one knee, and a hush fell over their small celebratory group. The sounds of everyone else faded into the background. This time Jack and Riley reached for each other's hands at the same time.

"Hayley Campbell-Hayes, will you marry me?"

She didn't even hesitate, said yes, and he slipped the ring on her finger, and then swept her up in a hug before kissing her. Donna and Sandra moved closer, Jim was crying, Donna couldn't seem to let Hayley or Logan go. Then Hayley was in front of them, with tears bright in her eyes.

"Daddy? Pappa?" she asked.

Something hot and wet slid down Riley's face, and he dashed it away.

"I love you so much," he said, his voice broken, and then he and Jack held out their free hands, and she moved into their circle of love, and they hugged, Hayley shifted a little in their hold, tugging Logan in as well.

"We need to FaceTime Mom and Dad," Logan said to Hayley, with Connor telling everyone he'd recorded the proposal.

That was it, then.

Hayley Campbell-Hayes was getting married to the boy she'd loved since she was ten.

Back in their room, after the celebration dinner, Riley was quiet, and Jack was equally subdued. The emotions today had been a rollercoaster of pride and love and he didn't know about Jack, but Riley felt wrung out. They stripped for bed, and climbed in at the same time, hugging. Riley was done with emotions, but he had one more thing to say.

"Thank you," he said, and that seemed like such a small number of words to explain what was in his heart. "For Hayley, and Max, and the twins, and for being mine." There, that added something else.

Jack rolled Riley onto his back and sprawled on him, kissing him. They didn't have to say words to love each other, but sometimes a thank you had to be given in words. Simple, gentle words that meant everything.

"Thank you, back," Jack said.

"I love you."

Jack smiled into a kiss, "Always," he repeated. "I'll always love you." And then he couldn't resist teasing Riley it seemed. "Even when you burn the bacon, I'll still love you."

"Always?"

"Yeah Riley, always."

BREAKFAST WAS A NOISY AFFAIR, AND RILEY WAS PLEASED THAT they'd managed to snag a private room, because he doubted their brand of celebration would go down well with the snooty clientele of this place.

Connor was on his third plate of bacon and eggs, a boy after Jack's heart, while Lexie was staring enraptured at a notebook Hayley had of ideas for her wedding. Hayley, Donna, Sandra, and Lexie were huddled around it as if it held the answers to the mysteries of the universe. Logan had decided to sit at the other end where there was more in the way of sanity.

But, was it just Riley who wished he were down there looking at wedding ideas? Neither Logan nor Hayley had said where they were getting married, but he hoped, right inside, that the wedding would be at the D. He could imagine the same beauty that Eden had created for their wedding, but instead of him and Jack it would be Hayley and Logan.

It wasn't his place to say anything; he wasn't going to interfere. He would stay here with the guys and play his part which was that of a hands-off dad who did things as paying for the wedding and giving his daughter away.

Wait. What about Jack? Maybe she'd want Jack to give her away. Or both of them.

Jesus, I am losing my mind over this. It's a wedding. It's one day.

"Uncle Jack, Riley?" Logan asked, and Riley snapped back to reality and realized Jack had to do the same. He and Jack exchanged rueful glances, and Riley wondered if Jack had been thinking about the same things. "Hayley and I were thinking we'd like to have the wedding at the D, if that was okay?"

"Of course, we'd love that," Jack said before Riley could.

"Yes," Riley added. Just in case Logan thought Jack hadn't been clear.

"And we were thinking…" He glanced down at the table to Hayley who was talking about colors. "Of a Christmas wedding, this year."

Jack held out a hand, and Logan took it to shake. "We can do that," he said.

And like that, not only were Hayley and Logan getting married, it was happening on Christmas on the D.

Max was the hardest sell about Hayley and Logan because his concept of marriage wasn't really formed. He understood a daddy, a pappa, a sister and a brother. He even seemed to understand the connection between his daddies and their parents, but weddings? Not so much.

So Hayley began calling it a big party, and he seemed more on board with that. Logan was spending more time at the ranch, and Riley noticed that a lot of that was spent attempting to connect to Max through the horses, and with the twins over photography and ballet.

"You think Logan will draw the line at wearing tights?" Jack smirked as he and Riley sat on the porch, feet up with a beer, watching Logan help Lexie with lifts in the yard. Hayley was on the fence smiling and laughing as Logan and Lexie performed a complicated set of moves that ended with Logan sprawled on the ground and a cackling Lexie sitting on his chest. Through all of it, Connor was taking photos, and Max had wandered into the scene and sat on the fence by Hayley.

"I think if Lexie asked him he probably would."

"True."

They watched some more. "You excited for Hayley's first day?" Jack asked, quieter, so it was just between them.

Hayley was starting at CH tomorrow in a formal intern position, not just as holiday experience. She'd be learning the floor, and actually be assigned to a team. Of course, she wasn't a normal intern, after all, one day CH would be hers to run for the family. She was working with JJ and Edward who were an effective and solid presence at CH. They had been there for several years now, married each other and had cut ties with Josiah Harrold, who Riley heard wasn't in the best of health. It seemed as if he'd overdone the drinking and smoking, and was paying the price, but at seventy-five he'd done well not to have someone like Riley stab him with a pitchfork.

"Yeah, I am, and nervous. She could hate it, I know she won't, but she might."

Jack raised his eyebrow, and Riley sighed. With just that small movement Jack told him he was an idiot, and he knew it.

He leaned farther back in his seat, feeling sleepy, soaking in the warmth of the day and the laughter of his children.

"You going to sleep, old man?" Jack teased and poked at his side.

"I'm forty-two, not forty-five like you, *old man.*"

The poking turned to tickling, which turned to Riley shaking his beer and pouring it all over Jack.

It was okay though. Showering together after the kids went to bed was one hell of a lot of fun.

CHAPTER 21

*J*ack couldn't have stayed away from CH even if he tried. He was drawn to the place to see their daughter working, but he didn't want to make it obvious. So he slunk by Kathy without saying a word, only exchanging wry smiles, and slid into Riley's office, closing the door and pulling the blind.

"What took you so long?" Riley teased from his desk. "It's been at least an hour since she started."

Jack tilted the blind a little so he could get a good look out to the desks beyond. "How's she doing?"

Riley joined him at the blinds and rested his chin on Jack's shoulder.

"Well, she knows where the coffee machine is, and Edward explained that we use red folders for research, blue for active investigations, and that green and yellow indicate active sites. I saw her writing it down very diligently, even though she already knew that. She didn't stop him once, because, and this is her words to me in the car, *I don't want anyone to think I know more than them about the office.*

"She hugged me in the elevator and then said I wasn't to hug her in the office, or talk to her, or even look at her."

Jack couldn't help laughing at that. "How will you manage that?"

Riley huffed. "Well, how would *you* manage it?"

"Poor Riley. Do you remember the day she helped you choose the folder colors? What was she? Thirteen?"

"Yep, but she sat there and listened to JJ explaining and didn't interrupt once."

"What will she do today?"

"More of the same, coffee runs, filing, the same kind of thing any intern does when they first come in, and then when she's ready she'll take on her own caseload of projects. JJ is taking her under his wing, apparently."

Jack glanced back at Riley and frowned. "You're sure?" He was skeptical about JJ showing Hayley the ropes, even if it had been four or so years since JJ had joined Riley's company, moved in with Edward and had become part of the CH team. Riley had said then that he'd be stupid to let Edward leave, and JJ had a whole lifetime of knowledge. He'd been right, the two of them had fitted in nicely at CH. He didn't know why he was suddenly feeling like that; after all, he'd given Riley the benefit of the doubt that he'd changed way back, so why not JJ?

"I wish it was me showing her," Riley admitted. "I think I'm jealous."

It hit Jack right then that this was what he was feeling. He wanted Riley to be Hayley's mentor, to show her the business, to be there for her.

But he couldn't. Eventually, she would be sitting in this office, and she needed to learn different perspectives.

"JJ will do well with her," Jack said, with confidence in his voice, "and you'll keep an eye on her."

Riley pressed a kiss to the side of Jack's neck. "Always."

JACK GOT BACK HOME AND WENT STRAIGHT TO HIS HORSES. HE couldn't help Hayley at work, had to trust that everything would go as well as her studies had done. He'd worried about that and it had all been unfounded. Their daughter was out in the big, bad world now and he had no control over that.

"She doing okay?" Robbie asked from a stall, leaning on the wood and looking at Jack with a know-it-all expression on his face. "Were you worrying for nothing, Pappa?"

Jack shoved him lightly. "You wait until one of your two leaves home, when Louise goes to college, or gets engaged, and then come smirking to me."

Robbie grinned, "Louise is never leaving the house," he said.

They worked for a long time, just like every other day, and when Vaughn joined them, Jack felt every small bit of tension leaving him. They worked long and hard, Jack ending the day at the school, with the horse program, getting his hands dirty.

"I don't want to worry you," Janet said. She was one of the new carers who accompanied the children from a local school. No sentence starting like that would end up well, and Jack tensed.

"What is it?"

"Mitchell is missing. He was here, and he's gone." She was checking against a clipboard, struggling to corral the kids, not used to the different ways in which they enjoyed the riding school.

Jack didn't panic. Mitchell was on the spectrum like Max, and he loved one thing more than any other when he was here.

"It's okay; he'll be in the stables. I'll go get him."

He'd learned so much over the years with this school, how to talk, when to talk, when not to talk, and Mitchell liked it when he hummed. Jack didn't even realize he hummed, not until Mitchell patted his face and smiled at him a few months ago.

He found him cleaning the stall, methodically working in small strips, and waited until Mitchell noticed him. He was non-verbal and struggled with communication, but his smile? It was beautiful. Jack held up the notebook he always had with him when he was at the school, the cards with images on them, and he held up the one for Mitchell, a picture of the bus that took them home.

Mitchell never argued, he placed the shovel very carefully by the wall and then dipped his head to scurry past Jack, bumping elbows with him as they passed. He didn't like to be touched or watched, unless it was on his terms. He was eighteen, just about to drop out of the education system and into adult care. One day Max would be at this point, thankfully not for a couple more years, but what happened to kids when they became adults?

"You know we could use Mitchell's help here," Liam said, standing next to Jack, his thumbs in his belt loops. Jack didn't think he was joking either, and maybe they could somehow work with young adults on the spectrum, offer them part-time jobs, work with carers and form some kind of program.

"What if we—?"

"Already on it boss," Liam interrupted.

"With a—?"

"I have a guy coming in to talk it through, offering placements, wanted to hand you the completed investigation, but yeah, I'd like to run with it if I could."

Liam was his second at the school, the man who ran things when Jack was working with Robbie, training, or on the breeding program. He shouldn't have to check with Jack about something like this, nor ask if it was okay to run with something that would be so good. He was working with Kyle at Legacy, running the school, and he was as intrinsically a part of the D as Jack was.

Jack made a decision, right there and then, and held out a hand, which Liam took, looking confused.

"Consider yourself promoted to manager of this place."

"Jack—"

"Keep doing what you're doing, count me in for my usual work here, but you take over, make decisions, follow your instincts. Work with Darren on the accounts, budgets. You want it?"

Liam was lost for words; then he shook Jack's hand firmly. "God, yes."

CHAPTER 22

*R*iley stood back and admired the sketch. "See," he began and tapped the design he'd drawn up for a house for Hayley and Logan. "Three bedrooms, all with bathrooms, a kitchen/diner, a living room—"

"They're having a 'living room'?" Jack teased.

Riley looked affronted. "Every house should have a special room to sit in with company."

"Okay then, carry on."

"So anyway, another room for family, and a loft room here." He tapped the top of the house emphatically.

"You're sure this is what they want?" Jack asked, some of that doubt he'd expressed when Riley first proposed the wedding gift creeping in. He wanted to do this for Hayley, give her a place that was hers on D land, and no, it wasn't because he couldn't bear the thought of her moving away. Or, yes, maybe it was that, but still, they had the money and the land, and they could make something special for them.

"It's what we can give them."

"What about Josh and Logan's office?"

Riley had considered that, "We could add something to

the ranch, offices. He scribbled an 'X' on the map of the ranch. "Right there, near the school."

Jack placed a hand over Riley's. "Riley, stop a minute."

Riley tried to move his hand, but Jack was clearly not letting it go. "What?" he asked, not recalling why was there a need for Jack to be all calming influence on him.

"Let's talk to Hayley, and Logan eh? Before we go on planning out the rest of their lives."

That hurt, right inside Riley. He wanted Jack to think this was a good thing, the best kind of wedding present, and something that Riley could do.

"They need somewhere to live," Riley said.

"And Logan wants to work for it, you know why."

"No, I don't, Hayley's fathers have money, an obscene amount of money that we could use to help them with a start in life."

"Riley." Jack curled his fingers around Riley's and tugged him, and Riley went with the flow, ending up being hugged and held close. "He wants to prove he can look after Hayley, is that so hard to understand? Will you respect him if he takes the money, or the house, or the freaking private jet you probably have on the list?"

"Of course I'll respect him, this is Hayley I'm thinking about."

"And so am I. Let them make their own way, we'll help them out as any kind of normal parents would, and give them some land here if they want to build a place, but Riley, let them do it for themselves."

Riley hated that, even at his most stubborn, Jack had this way of pushing through things enough for Riley to realize Jack was probably right. He loved that about Jack. He hated that about Jack.

"Fuck's sake," Riley muttered against Jack's shirt.

"So we look at their gift list, give them something from

there, and talk to them about how else we could help. Agreed?"

Riley sighed. "I don't suppose there is anything on the list that says a new house, or a private jet, or maybe an island in the Caribbean?"

Jack laughed and kissed Riley hard. "No," he said when they separated. "I doubt it."

They parted and Riley turned the page in his notebook. He wasn't ready to destroy the house he'd sketched, and maybe one day Hayley and Logan would want this place but at this moment he knew in his heart that Jack was right.

"Ready to pick her up and go?"

They were dress shopping this morning, something that normally filled both men with dread, but this was a wedding dress, and she wanted her dads to be there. There was a whole group of people wanting to be involved, and at first Riley had thought that it was too many but Hayley had family, extended family, and it was right that she wanted to share it. She'd asked both of them to give her away, and for that they needed fitting for suits, something he loved and Jack dreaded.

But anyway, the dress.

They picked Hayley up from work, and headed to the wedding dress place, a huge sprawling area that Hayley had to herself. The ceilings were low, the lighting bright and there were racks upon racks of dresses.

Alicia, the bridal consultant, introduced herself, there was champagne, canapés and a lot of laughter.

And only one dress, the first dress she picked. Riley didn't know much about dresses, waistlines, beading, or veils.

He just knew that seeing Hayley in the dress made him cry.

DINNER WAS NOISY; THEY'D GONE HOME AND LOGAN JOINED them, Jack teasing that he'd seen the dress and would Logan like to know what it looked like. The two of them went and sat on the porch post-dinner, which left just him and Hayley in the kitchen after the kids had gone to bed. They washed up, bumping arms, and finally, they gave up all pretense, and she walked into his arms and held onto him.

"Your momma would have loved to have been there," Riley said, emotion choking him. They had another letter for Hayley, which was why Jack had taken Logan outside. Was now a good time? He couldn't say, but the note on the front in Hayley's mom's handwriting was very clear, *for the day Hayley chooses her wedding dress.*

She knew as well, clinging to his hand when he handed it to her. They'd moved to Riley and Jack's room and sat on the bed, Riley tried to release her hold, but she wouldn't let go.

"Can you read it, dad?" she asked softly, the letter in her lap, untouched.

"I think maybe it's for you to read first," Riley insisted.

Hayley shook her head and handed him the letter. "She'd want to know that you were part of this."

Riley looked out the window a little desperately, hoping to will Jack back inside, but there was nothing he could do, and he sat on the bed next to her and took the paper. The seal wasn't as sticky as the earlier letters, and it was the penultimate letter, the only other one was for if Hayley had kids. A small package wrapped in tissue was inside the envelope, but he didn't unwrap it; that was for Hayley to do. Each time he thought of Lexie, the woman who'd given him Hayley, he was struck by a special kind of grief, that Hayley wouldn't have her mom for the special times. So even beginning to read the letter he was a mess.

"Dearest Hayley," he began, and coughed to clear his tight throat. "I can't believe that my little girl is now choosing a wedding dress. I'm not exactly sure what to write here, because I didn't have a wedding," Riley stopped, and grief flooded him. He hadn't even known that Lexie was pregnant, but he'd treated her wrong, and he carried that with him every day. They'd never had a wedding, not like his and Jack's.

What would he have done? Would he have married her if she'd told him? He tried to imagine the bastard he'd been, the kid who'd used to drink to excess and whore about, and hoped to hell that maybe he would have done the right thing if he'd got a girl pregnant.

Hayley linked hands with him again. "Go on," she encouraged, and he realized he'd stopped.

"Okay," he cleared his throat again and settled his breathing. "I didn't have a wedding," he repeated, "but I had you, and that more than made up for any kind of special day with some man I'd fallen in love with. I hope the man you have met is good to you, treats you well. I hope he works hard, and you talk, and that he is everything you wished for. And for the dress, I hope that what you have makes you feel like the princess you always pretended to be as a child. There won't be a letter for your wedding day, because that should be the happiest day of your life, with no tears of grief.

Riley cleared his throat, pushing back the tears and then continued.

"There is a gift here for you, it's not an heirloom, but it's a present I bought that I would love for you to sew into your dress on your wedding day. You don't have to wear it, but to know it was with you, that would make me happy. As always, my darling, I love you, and I know that you looked absolutely beautiful today trying on dresses and veils." Riley couldn't help being choked, the lettering so familiar, and the link to the past so visceral. He passed the small wrapped gift to Hayley, and she opened the tissue paper to reveal a small pendant on a gold chain, a pale blue sapphire hanging from it.

"Oh," Hayley said, holding it up and watching the sapphire spin and catch the light. "Oh," she said again. "Momma."

Riley held his daughter close, until the grief became something else. Until it became a recognition that her mom would always be there for her, and that the necklace was her connection to family.

"I'll wear it, I won't sew it somewhere hidden," Hayley announced, and held the chain close to her heart. "I won't," she replied fiercely.

Jack and Logan were in the kitchen waiting for them, and Logan held back a moment, allowing Jack to hug Hayley.

Then Logan took Hayley's hand and led her outside to talk; to be alone. He was the man she would turn to at the end of things. Not him and Jack anymore, not for everything.

And that was just as it should be.

CHAPTER 23

The day of Hayley and Logan's wedding didn't start so well. There might have been the dress, and the cake, and a million other things that were really important, but that didn't mean things couldn't go wrong.

"Hayley's crying," Connor announced as he ran past Riley and Jack as if the hounds of hell were on his tail, slamming out of the kitchen and vanishing from sight.

When Lexie sauntered out after him she shook her head. "He can't handle a woman crying," she said with all the adulting an eleven-year-old could manage. Riley would have laughed, but all he could think was that Hayley was crying. "And Aunty Eden doesn't know what to do."

"Why is Hayley crying?" Jack asked before Riley could.

"Who knows." Lexie slumped at the table. Her sapphire blue bridesmaid's dress stuck out at an angle, and she smoothed it down. She'd been wearing it since this morning, and nothing Riley or Jack said could pry her out of it.

"Don't spill anything on your dress," Jack commented, as he had been doing all day, and then gestured for Riley to go first.

Hayley was crying, and maybe she needed her daddies.

Riley knocked on the door, even though it was ajar. He didn't want to go barreling into her room without giving her the chance to say go away.

Eden came to the door.

"I don't know what's wrong," she said. "But she wanted me to come and get you." She hugged Riley briefly, and patted Jack on the chest and then went the way of Connor and Lexie.

They exchanged brief looks of worry, and Riley didn't have to know Jack as well as he did to see that they were thinking the same thing. That maybe she was regretting this? Maybe she didn't want to marry Logan?

She was sitting on her bed in a robe, her long blonde hair all twisted up in the complicated knot that Eden had helped her with. No hairdressers for Hayley, or anyone to do makeup, today for her was all about doing things with Eden. She glanced up when they walked in and she wasn't crying now, but she looked lost.

Riley sat down beside her; Jack took the stool that sat in front of the vanity, impossibly huge on the tiny thing.

"What's wrong, Hays?" Riley started when Jack looked at him and nodded.

"Mom didn't write me a letter for today," she said, and twisted her hands in her lap.

"Oh sweetheart, is that is what's upsetting you?"

"No," she said, "she said all she wanted in the last one, told me she didn't want me to cry on my wedding day. You know that." She fiddled with the chain around her neck with the sapphire, twisting it around her finger and holding it close.

"I know, but maybe it would have been better if she had," this from Jack.

"No, it's nothing to do with Mom, or it is, but it isn't." She bowed her head, and there were fresh tears.

Riley's heart broke seeing Hayley so upset. "Hayley, if you're having second thoughts about the wedding, sweetheart."

"We had plans," Hayley sobbed. Jack stood and closed the door, locking it so there were no accidental interruptions. Something was seriously wrong here. "We were going to get a place near his work, just a small place, and I would commute from there when I was in the office. We were going to have a garden, and go for walks, and maybe get a dog, because Logan can take a dog to his office, and we were going to sit on our sofa and watch TV and cuddle and he said we could travel the world, and visit places we'd never seen, and we were waiting..." she sobbed again.

"Hayley, calm down honey." Jack reached for her hands and held them, and Riley put an arm over her shoulder. "Talk to us."

"Is it Logan?" Riley felt this rush of protective-dad, and when Jack caught his eye he knew he was feeling the same. The kids and each other were everything. "Did he do something?"

"No," she sobbed, "Yes. No."

"I'll kill him," Jack said and made to stand up.

She held out a hand. "No, Pappa, it was both of us."

"You're not making any sense," Riley said.

"It's all ruined," she murmured, and leaned into Riley. "And I don't know how to fix it. No," she looked up at them then, her expression stricken, "I don't want to fix it."

Silence.

Then Jack cleared his throat, imagining the worst. "Okay, so I'm not killing Logan, but are we canceling the wedding Hayley? It's okay, you don't have to worry, but guests are arriving so I'd need to go out and—"

"No, I need to talk to Logan. I don't care if it's bad luck, can someone find Logan?" Jack stood, and nodded, he would find Logan, but she reached out and stopped him. "Pappa, don't hurt him, he hasn't done anything wrong. I just need to talk to him."

Riley held Hayley close when Jack left. "You can talk to us," he said, hoping that would be enough to get through to her, but she shook her head sadly.

"I want to talk to Logan first; I need to."

"Okay."

Jack came back with a concerned Logan, dressed to the nines in a dark gray suit with a sapphire tie the same color as the bridesmaids' dresses.

As soon as he saw Hayley, he rushed to her, "Hayley, what's wrong, please…"

Riley released his hold, and left the room to stand with Jack, but not before he sent Logan his best daddy-frown, to which Logan's eyes widened. Riley shut the door behind him.

"I don't know what Logan did," he whispered, "but I will kill him if he's hurt her."

He expected Jack to be torn, but he was in full on Pappa-bear mode and just growled. Everything was quiet in the room, and Riley itched with the need to go in and see what was happening. Josh and Anna arrived.

"Eden said Hayley is talking to Logan," Josh said, "what happened? Is the wedding off?"

Jack shrugged at his brother, and Riley couldn't find the words to say anything.

The door opened, and Riley was the first one in, the others close behind. Far from crying, Hayley was smiling, hesitant, a little unsure, but smiling. Logan was as well, although he was pale. They held hands, the two of them, and it didn't seem they were contemplating calling the wedding off.

"Logan?" Josh asked.

Logan tilted his chin and hugged Hayley into his side.

"Change of plans," he said, and Hayley looked at him adoringly.

"Is the wedding canceled?" Anna asked. "What happened?"

"No," Logan smile widened. "Not a change of wedding plans, of our plans. You tell them, Hayley."

Riley stared at his daughter, thought he saw more tears, but she was smiling, like Logan.

"I'm pregnant," she said.

The room went quiet, and then Anna stepped forward, as if she'd almost expected the news, worked it out from them standing there like idiots grinning. She hugged them, and then it hit Riley and Jack and Josh all at the same time, their kids were pregnant.

The hugs were hard, and Riley was lost for words again, unable to do anything except hold Hayley close.

Because hell, he and Jack were going to be grandparents.

THE WEDDING WAS BEAUTIFUL.

But Riley was sure he missed so much. As the moment they said I do, because he was blindly reaching for Jack's hand. Or the point when he was supposed to turn and follow husband and wife down the aisle between the decorated chairs, but couldn't move because he was so overwhelmed.

And happy.

So happy.

The wedding was under a large awning decorated with fairy lights and winter roses, and even though it was still warm outside there was the feel of Christmas in the soft light. He remembered teasing Jack about which side he'd sit, bride or groom; he remembered Jack kissing the smile from him and laughing.

He recalled the photos, and the cheers, and the vows

where Hayley said just a few words. That was what got to him the most.

I promise I will always love you as much as my dad and pappa love each other.

But the fact that their daughter, in her gorgeous dress, which draped her in lace and voile, was pregnant?

That was all he could think about. How was she? Was she well? How did they know for sure? When was the baby due?

"Oh God," he took the nearest seat. Jack sat next to him and held his hand and they didn't talk at first. They simply sat and watched Hayley and Logan talking to guests and every so often Riley saw Hayley touch her belly, as if she had to reassure herself of the life that was inside her.

They'd said they wanted to keep the news quiet for a while, just their parents, but Riley was nearly bursting with love and the need to shout it from the rooftops.

"How many people do you want to tell right now?" Jack said under his breath.

"Everyone. Like, I want to take out an ad in the *Dallas Morning News* or something."

"I think I'm in shock," Jack added.

Riley shoulder bumped his husband. "Grandpa Jack," he whispered and then bussed his cheekbone. "And Grandpa Riley."

"Has a nice ring to it," Jack turned his head so that this time the kiss was on his lips.

The party went on into the night, and Hayley and Logan left for their honeymoon, a week on the same island where Riley and Jack had been when they'd first heard the news of Hayley even existing. Some things worked well in a full circle.

The kids were in bed; the family had left, all except Josh and Anna. The four of them sat on the porch, Jack and Josh nursing beers, Riley with a whiskey and Anna with the remains of a bottle of champagne.

"Well," she began and lifted her glass. "We should toast to a happy, healthy pregnancy and to the fact we're all getting old."

They all raised their glasses to the toast, and then sat back and stared into the night.

"We should have seen this coming," Josh said.

"Logan/Hayley was always going to happen," Anna mused out loud. "And now a baby."

"A baby," Riley added softly.

"Yeah," Jack agreed.

A wedding and a baby all in one day.

This family never did things by halves.

he call came at three am, the absolute worst time for
calls, and Jack awoke immediately, fear gripping him
the same way with any middle of the night call. All he could
think was that this was about Hayley, but she was only thirty-
seven weeks pregnant. She'd been healthy so far, but the
diabetes was always a concern. They were all due to meet up
tomorrow to celebrate his and Riley's fifteenth wedding
anniversary, and Hayley had planned it all despite her advanced
pregnancy and still working part-time at CH on JJ's team.

"What's wrong?" he asked, instead of his normal hello.

"Uncle Jack, I'm at the hospital." Logan didn't sound
panicked, but the baby wasn't due yet, so this had to be an
emergency, right?

"What's wrong?" he asked. Riley sat up next to him.

"Is that Logan? What's happened?" Riley asked, and Jack
shushed him with a wave of his hand.

"Hayley had a migraine, and they took her to the hospital,
nothing to worry about, but they want to keep her in for
observation."

"We're coming now," Jack said, and both he and Riley scrambled off the bed.

He didn't even end the call, but when he checked, Logan had gone. They made it to the hospital in silence.

"It's too soon isn't it?" Riley said.

"I don't know," Jack answered. Because he didn't. Yes, he knew that babies were nine months from conception, but he didn't know if only reaching thirty-seven weeks was good or bad. He'd read so much in the way of conflicting evidence, trawling his way through the stack of baby books Riley had bought when the twins were due to arrive.

The hospital was quiet, but then at four a.m. it would be, Josh and Anna were already there, sipping hot coffee in the waiting room.

"It's okay," Anna said as soon as Jack and Riley walked in. "They suspect pre-eclampsia, but she's in the best place and if she has to have the baby now, then that's fine."

Jack sat in the nearest chair, the cheap plastic grumbling under his weight.

"What can we do?" Riley asked, looking from them to the door marked *Staff only*. "Pre-eclampsia is bad, right?"

The door opened, and a disheveled Logan walked out, his blue eyes bloodshot, his dark hair sticking up as if he'd been twisting his hands into it.

"She's okay. They're looking to induce her because her blood pressure is too high, and her liver function is messed up. Not to mention her sugar levels are all over the place." He scrubbed at his eyes. "I need to go back in."

"Logan?" Jack called after him as he opened the door.

"Yeah?"

"Tell her we all love her."

"I will."

The night turned to morning, and the mood between the

four of them had lightened with good reports delivered with every visit from Logan.

Jack and Riley went to find something to eat, then Josh and Anna took their turn, and there was a long time when there was no news of anything, and lots of texts back home to reassure the rest of the family that everything was okay. Eden arrived a little before midday.

"I managed to persuade everyone that only one of us should visit," she sat next to Riley, pulling out her phone. She typed out a message and sent it, then sat back. "I've told everyone that everything is fine. I'm not lying, am I?"

Jack shook his head. "We haven't heard anything for the last couple of hours."

The five of them sat in silence, until Eden went for a coffee run, and a pediatric nurse stopped to chat with them. She didn't have anything to do with Hayley but she was interested to know who they were waiting for and reassured them that she was sure everything was okay.

All Jack could think was that it had now been three hours without news, and next to him Riley was getting twitchy. Jack was going to give it ten more minutes, until his watch passed noon, and then he was going to go all irate grandparent on someone's ass, because they needed to know.

Eleven-fifty-seven passed to fifty-eight, and just as he was ready to stand, the door opened, and a flushed Logan nearly fell into the room.

"A boy, we've had a boy, and Hayley is fine, Hayley is beautiful, and you have to come in, but you can't, and I'll come back for you." He spun and went back in, but the door swung open again. "Six-pounds-eleven, a boy. Did I say it was a boy?"

And then he left.

"Six-eleven is a good weight," Anna mused.

"We have a grandson," Josh elbowed Jack in the side.

"Oh my god," Riley murmured.

But Jack had no words that he wanted to share, because if he opened his mouth he would shout out with joy and then would likely cry.

Cowboys didn't cry.

Except for the tear that slid out unbidden as he buried his face in Riley's hair.

But, one tear? Hell, he was a granddaddy, and his daughter was fine, so that one tear was allowed.

MASON CHRISTOPHER CAMPBELL WAS BEAUTIFUL. FROM THE tip of his tiny button nose, to his wispy dark hair, to the tiniest of fists that curled as he fed. Only three hours old and he'd already stolen the hearts of everyone in the room. Jack took a couple of photos, even though Hayley said she was exhausted. Maybe he wouldn't send them to anyone, but he wanted to capture the absolute perfection of his new grandson.

"I'm sorry about the party," Hayley said, sounding tired.

Jack shook his head, holding Riley's hand tight. "You gave us the best gift."

When Mason had finished nursing, Logan held him for a short while and the love the new dad had for the baby and his wife was obvious. He was so completely proud of how his little family was doing, and Jack knew they had to give the new parents some space. Hayley was coming home in a couple of days, they wanted to keep an eye on her kidneys and her sugars, but her diabetes had been steady and well-taken care of and they were happy to say that by Saturday she would be home.

Jack kissed her goodbye, pulled Logan into a hug, and then held baby Mason for the shortest of times, before passing him to Riley, who then passed him onto Josh and

Anna. Eden was in charge of corralling everyone, and Jack didn't want that job.

They stopped on the way home at a toy store, but what did you buy a baby less than a day old?

When the debate was between a near life-size baby giraffe and an entire litter of stuffed Dalmatians, they realized things were getting out of hand.

Of course, carrying the five-foot giraffe to the car, and then fitting it in the car was hilarious, given Jack and Riley were both on very little sleep and at the same time hyped-up on coffee and love.

At home, Jack showed Connor and Lexie their new nephew, and he and Riley talked to Max about the baby in Hayley's tummy coming out to say hello.

And then, somehow it was time for bed, and Jack couldn't sleep. He tossed and turned and stared at the wall. Until Riley's arm came across his chest and held him tightly. He turned in his husband's hold, and they cuddled for the longest time.

And finally, Jack slept.

EPILOGUE

*M*ason's fifth birthday coincided with Jack and Riley's twentieth wedding anniversary, and the party was huge.

They'd lost Toby, Riley's black lab, the year before, but the twins had a dog each, not much older than puppies, so the ranch wasn't without a dog. In fact, Buttons and Henry were fighting over a chew stick that Jack was holding just out of their reach. Of course, he ended up on the floor with them, and then Mason joined in, as did Mason's younger sister Diana who'd just turned three, and Riley finally went over to help, extricating Jack from the two toddlers and the puppies with ease.

"You'll have to help me up." Jack held up a hand.

"I'm not falling for that again." Riley crouched next to his husband. "You are not pulling me down so we can make out on the ground."

Jack pouted then grinned, rolling to a stand and brushing himself down. "I was never going to do that," he said, but Riley could tell he was lying.

Hand in hand they followed children and puppies back to

the party, catching up with Diana and Jack swinging her up into his arms.

Jack let Diana down, and she toddled over to Hayley and the puppies, and the rest of their family waiting to start the anniversary/birthday party.

Their family was bigger.

Max had his own apartment attached to the house, and was mostly self-sufficient with some care and had the biggest collection of Thomas figures Riley had ever seen. He was happy in his own world, and loved his family, and that was all they'd ever wanted for the boy who'd stolen their hearts.

Connor was at college studying geology like his sister, but his real talent lay in Math which, God knew where he got that from, as Jack often said.

Lexie went full time to a performing arts school. She was born to be on stage and would always be Jack and Riley's spitfire of a daughter.

But at the core of it all, the melding of two families, the children, the marriages, the loves and all the trials that came with *family*, were Riley and Jack.

They walked toward the party area, with balloons and cake and face painting, and Riley's heart was so full he didn't think he'd have room for more people to love.

Then Connor came over to them, as if he'd been waiting for them, holding hands with someone that Riley couldn't see at first, half hidden behind Connor. As they drew closer, Riley recognized Elliot, a kid from Connor's school, an old friend who had clearly become more.

"Dad, Pappa, I want you to meet Elliot. My boyfriend."

And somehow, Riley's heart expanded a little more and made room for someone else, and next to him Jack was probably feeling the same way. They talked a little; Elliot and Connor seemed besotted with each other, and it was so lovely to see. They went off to find food, and Jack turned to Riley to say something.

He was smiling widely, and Riley stopped walking.

Jack didn't look any older than the day Riley had asked him to come to the offices of Hayes Oil. Yes he was gray at the temples, yes the laugh lines were deeper, but in Jack's blue eyes he was still that man that Riley had fallen for twenty years ago.

"What's wrong?" Jack cradled Riley's face.

They kissed gently, the brush of lips and the familiar taste of each other, just like home.

"I love you," Riley said, hoping the words meant more to Jack each time he said them. "I've always loved you, and I always will."

"I love you, too," Jack said, softly, "I've always loved you, and yeah, I always will."

And like that, hand in hand, they joined everyone else and celebrated what they had worked so hard to make.

Family.

THE END

Crooked Tree Ranch on the banks of the Blackfoot river, is home to the Todd brothers and extended family. This best selling series has secrets, lies, love, the dude ranch, horses, and above all, family

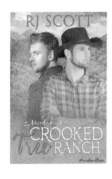

When a cowboy, meets the guy from the city, he can't know how much things will change.

On the spur of the moment, with his life collapsing around him, Jay Sullivan answers an ad for a business manager with an expertise in marketing, on a dude ranch in Montana.

With his sister, Ashley, niece, Kirsten and nephew, Josh, in tow, he moves lock stock and barrel from New York to Montana to start a new life on Crooked Tree Ranch.

Foreman and part owner of the ranch, ex-rodeo star

Nathaniel 'Nate' Todd has been running the dude ranch, for five years ever since his mentor Marcus Allen became ill.

His brothers convince him that he needs to get an expert in to help the business grow. He knows things have to change and but when the new guy turns up, with a troubled family in tow - he just isn't prepared for how much.

Book 5, Second Chance Ranch, the last in the series, coming 2018

The Red Dirt Heart is one of N.R. Walker's best-selling series. Where the Outback Australian landscape is its own character, and there's blistering heat under the summer sun and in the bedroom. With over 3880 ratings on Goodreads, do yourself a favor and meet Charlie and Travis and the rest of the crew at Sutton Station.

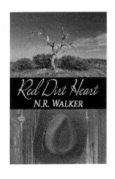

Welcome to Sutton Station: One of the world's largest working farms in the middle of Australia – where if the animals and heat don't kill you first, your heart just might.

Charlie Sutton runs Sutton Station the only way he knows how; the way his father did before him. Determined to keep his head down and his heart in check, Charlie swears the red dirt that surrounds him – isolates him – runs through his veins.

American agronomy student Travis Craig arrives at Sutton Station to see how farmers make a living from one of the harshest environments on earth. But it's not the barren, brutal and totally beautiful landscapes that capture him so completely, it's the man with the red dirt heart.

Made in the USA
Columbia, SC
22 March 2018